ROCK 'n ROLL HEAVEN

Shawn Inmon

Rock 'n Roll Heaven

By Shawn Inmon

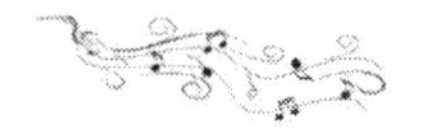

Cover Design/Interior Design: Linda Boulanger
www.TellTaleBookCovers.weebly.com

Published by Pertime Publishing

Also available in eBook publication

PRINTED IN THE UNITED STATES OF AMERICA

Dedication

For Joni, my very first "first reader"

and

For SK, for firing my imagination

Jimi Hendrix leaned his chair back, eyes shut, the wide, floppy brim of his hat drooping low over his forehead. His fingers flew over the strings and frets of his famously flipped Fender Stratocaster. He bit his lip in concentration, looking for something; a new sound, a new… anything.

He slammed the chair down in frustration as he realized that the riff that had appeared in his head had rematerialized as nothing more than a slight variation of what he had done in *Little Wing*. He looked across the table at Gram Parsons, who was leaning his cheek against the neck of his guitar, shaking his head.

"Nothing?" Gram said?

"Nothing new," Jimi said.

Across the room, Bob Marley stood and stretched, rubbing his eyes.

"Why?" Bob said in his Jamaican lilt. "Why bring us all together, then keep us from writing, from creating anything new? It's what we do. It's who we are."

"I think," Jimi said, "this isn't heaven at all."

Chapter One

Jimmy 'Guitar' Velvet lifted his arm straight up, held it there for one beat, then two, obeying his own inner metronome, then whipped it around in his last windmill jam of the night. Sweat flew off him, splattering and soaking into the rough wooden planks of the dance floor. He kneeled at the front of the tiny stage like it was an altar and coaxed every last bit of fuzz out of his Fender Stratocaster.

It was February 3rd, 1993, and Jimmy was celebrating his birthday. Like almost every birthday in his adult life, he was marking it onstage. Jimmy was still tall and lean at 44, wearing a black Ramones *Gabba Gabba Hey* T-shirt, faded Levi 501s and black biker boots. He looked every bit the aging rock star, even though he'd never actually been a star.

The bartender had made his "last call for alcohol" announcement ("You don't have to go home, but you can't stay here") fifteen minutes earlier. Only two dancers were left, propping each other up in a drunken embrace, unaware that the last slow dance had been *Home Sweet Home* three songs ago.

Jimmy turned to the rest of The Black Velvets and waited for them to join him in the final chord crash of *Free Bird*. They finished with a flourish, and the final note echoed off the back wall. Jimmy stepped to the microphone. There was tepid applause from the six or seven paying customers who had stuck around until closing time.

"Thank you very much! I'm Jimmy 'Guitar' Velvet and this is The Loudest Bar Band in the World, The Black Velvets. Good night!"

A few years earlier, Jimmy might have tried to remember the name of the town they were playing, so he could say

“Goodnight, Walla Walla,” or “See ya next time, Longview,” but no longer. In those glory days, The Black Velvets would set down their instruments, put their arms around each other and take a bow, basking in the reflected glory of an appreciative crowd. Back then, Jimmy saved a killer song or two for the end, knowing they would give in and do an encore.

One drunken straggler weaved toward the stage, Pabst Blue Ribbon bottle held high, yelling “Rock ‘n Roll! Whoooo!”

There would be no encore tonight.

They were playing The Eagles Nest, a bar owned by a former mechanic named Sal. In all the years Jimmy had played the Nest, he never understood how people found it, or where they came from, but when the sun went down and the sound went up, people materialized. The Eagles Nest had actually been Sal's auto garage before he decided that selling watery drinks was an easier living than fixing carburetors. Neon signs for Rainier, Heidelberg and Olympia beers covered the walls. Backstage, one could still see half-peeled posters on the wall that advertised tools and other things marketed to car repair shops.

If you knew where to look, just to the right of the Wurlitzer jukebox, you could find a cluster of three bullet holes, the result of a legendary bar fight in 1978. The Nest had the potential to be quaint, or charming, but it wasn’t. It was a dump, typical of the places The Black Velvets played.

Jimmy set his Strat in his guitar stand and turned to find Rollie waiting at the edge of the stage with a towel and a Coke. Jimmy sat down on a old wooden chair in what passed for a backstage. Before he had toweled off and drained half the Coke, J.J.’s drum kit was down and Mark and Drew’s guitar and bass were tucked away.

A case for everything and everything in its case.

As much as The Eagles Nest sucked, tonight's sets had been good. Tight. This most recent incarnation of The Black Velvets had been together for almost a year. Everyone in the band but Rollie was at least twenty years younger than Jimmy, but that didn’t matter. They were starting to become a real band.

Thirty years experience had taught Jimmy what he privately called 'The Evolution Of A Rock Band.'

It started with a bunch of guys hanging around, jamming together and playing the music they loved. You sounded like crap, but no one cared because everyone liked each other. If you stuck it out and landed a few gigs, you started to understand each other's styles. Over time, you came together like one big happy family.

After a few months or a year or two, you got to the peak, where everyone knew everyone else, the instruments working together as if guided by one mind. If your band was ever going to get past playing the Eagles Nests of the world, and make it big, that's when it would happen.

If your crew didn't catch that big break, though, the wheels started coming off the Stardom Express. All the little things that never seemed to bother you before—drug problems, supersized egos, bad hygiene, and vocal girlfriends offering, unasked for, dippy ideas on "exactly what this band needs to do to make it" began to bug you. People began considering their options. For example, the rhythm section might hear of a band across town seeking a drummer and bass player. Pretty soon, the cycle began again. That was why there weren't many forty-four-year-old lead guitarists like Jimmy, sticking it out on the bar circuit.

Still dreaming the dream. Or so I tell myself. Do I really dream it anymore? Sure, sure.

Over the years, fourteen different lineups had played under The Black Velvets' banner. Jimmy would have forgotten how many, but Rollie kept track in a creased little notebook. *Why he keeps it, I don't know. Maybe some sense of morbid fascination.*

Two constants had been part of all those different lineups: Jimmy and Rollie. They had met during their sophomore year in high school, when they were regular old Jimmy Andrzejewski and Rollie Klein. The Beatles had invaded, and every girl in school was fantasizing about the Fab Four. Jimmy and Rollie did not overlook this trend.

His Uncle Bill had given Jimmy a real guitar for his tenth

birthday. It was his first love. He couldn't read music, but he took his allowance down to the record store every week and bought a new 45. He sat in his bedroom and played along with *Oh, Boy* or *Wake Up, Little Susie* until he imagined that could play them just like Buddy Holly or Phil and Don Everly.

Until he observed the unique impact of rock musicians on his female peers, Jimmy'd never taken the music out of his bedroom. Jimmy thought that girls sighing over him would be very interesting, so he got the bright idea to form a band. He recruited Rollie, who had never before played an instrument, as the bass player. "All you've got to do is follow along with the drummer. It's easy," Jimmy had told him.

They recruited two buddies, both of whom were also interested in any reasonably legal activity with the potential to induce females to remove their undergarments, and thus the first edition of what would become The Black Velvets came into being. The name hadn't come easily. One or more members had—mercifully, in hindsight—rejected names like Jimmy and the Jim Tones, the Mossy Rockers, and The Bugs. They argued about it for weeks before resorting to heavy weaponry: they stole a bottle of whiskey from Rollie's dad, then locked themselves in Jimmy's garage until they figured it out. Although they passed out before they settled on a name, morning brought them massive headaches and an empty whiskey bottle staring at them with their new name: The Black Velvets.

They started out playing keggers in secluded locations where one could get by with copious underage drinking. They didn't get paid, aside from all the beer they could drink, but they learned three very important lessons. First: drinking lots of beer did not improve their music. Second: this deterioration in skill did not cause girls to love them less. Third: Rollie hadn't been bullshitting. He indeed lacked any performing musical talent.

Another kegger band in the area broke up during that time. Rollie knew the bass player, a lanky guy named Jon Averill. Jon was the bassist Rollie wasn't, but instead of quitting, Rollie became the roadie and stage manager. His genius for holding a sound system together with chewing gum and baling twine did far more for The Black Velvets than he ever could have with a bass guitar.

Jimmy and Rollie had been together ever since. Their friendship was the closest thing to a long-term relationship either one of them had ever experienced.

This latest incarnation of The Black Velvets was starting to gel. *If I'd found these guys fifteen years ago, we might have caught a couple of breaks, signed a record deal and be rich and famous now.* Of course, all the other guys in the band had been in elementary school fifteen years ago, but Jimmy tried not to dwell on that.

Jimmy liked to say that the only way he had changed over the years was that he had more gray hairs and far less hangovers. At times he wondered why he still played the rocker game, and usually concluded that it was about all he knew in life.

Tonight, at least, Jimmy did it in order to fill up the Magic Bus with fuel. This meant finding Sal and being paid, which was likelier at The Eagles Nest than at some gigs. Jimmy stood up off the little stool, winced at a crick in his back, and glimpsed himself through the spiderweb cracks in the nearby full-length mirror. With sweaty hair and two days' graying whiskers, the image in the mirror could have been that of his father, now twenty years dead. *By his early forties, Dad had married, had two kids, lived his life and died. By my early forties, I have played thousands of dives like this, made my hearing worse, and broken a long string of promises. Mostly to myself.*

What in the hell have I done with my life?

"Sold my soul for rock 'n roll," he muttered under his breath as he went to search for Sal to collect the money.

He tracked Sal down in the slimy little closet that was the backstage men's room at the 'Nest.

"How was the crowd tonight, Sal?"

Sal was somewhere in his sixties, with greasy grey hair

combed straight back. He still wore his old garage shirt and pants, including a faded red-on-yellow oval name patch. He was intimidating despite lack of size, with a presence that tended to keep trouble at bay. And if it didn't, the bat and the illegal scattergun under the bar had the rest covered. Sal shrugged. "It was all right. Nothin' special. After I pay you guys, I might maybe break even on the night. Next time around, we might need to renegotiate your fee."

Jimmy began to call bullshit, then caught himself. *You goombah, I know how much you charge for those weak-ass drinks. You've made a mint paying people like me barely enough to get to the next joint. You never just 'broke even' in your entire life. But yeah, you were busting my balls back when I still had a good future ahead of me, instead of too much past behind me. You're an equal opportunity prick to everybody.*

"Whatever, Sal. I'll give you a call when we're passing through again. It wouldn't be life on the road without a stop at the Nest."

Sal pulled out a leather wallet the size of a paperback book. He held it away from Jimmy and fished out two fifties and ten twenties. Jimmy nodded, climbed back onstage and started to pack his guitar and amp.

"Another fabulous night in the life of a glamorous rock 'n roll star, huh Jim?"

Jimmy didn't even look up from the cable he was looping. "Sho 'nuff, Rollie. Hey, I got an idea…why don't you go unlock the stage door and let a few of those groupies in I'm always reading about in *Rolling Stone*."

"Shit, man. I didn't know you were going to be in the mood, so I sent 'em all home disappointed."

With few variations, they'd had this conversation a thousand times.

Less than an hour later, the amps, instruments and sound board were loaded on the Magic Bus, idling in the back parking lot like a noisy locomotive. Rollie had named it that fifteen years ago, but the only magical thing about it was how it managed to log so many miles between engine rebuilds. The Magic Bus was a '59 school bus converted to the specific needs of a traveling rock band. Its exterior was a crazy quilt of its original yellow, primer gray and spray-painted graffiti. Storage space in the back held their equipment, with enough room left over so everyone had a little personal space inside. Personal space was a help, especially when one of The Black Velvets insisted on bringing a girlfriend on the road—or, more frequently, when a Black Velvet's lady friend insisted on traveling with the band.

For The Black Velvets, it was home.

Mark, Drew and J.J. climbed on board and settled into their spots while Jimmy and Rollie did one last stage walkthrough. It was all too easy to misplace cables, light boxes or duct tape. When you ran as close to the bone as The Black Velvets, you left no stray piece of equipment behind. By the time they got on the bus, Jimmy heard snoring from the back.

Jimmy smiled, shook his head and said, "They don't breed 'em like they used to, do they? We used to play all night and party all mornin'. Now they crash before we even roll out of the parking lot."

"True," Rollie said, "but that's why we look the way we do. When they're as old as we are, they'll still be beautiful. Nobody's accused us of that in a damn long time."

"I hope I die before I get old," Jimmy muttered.

For many of their years together, Jimmy and Rollie had partied with the best of them. And with the worst of them. They drank, smoked, injected, huffed or otherwise indulged in every excess they could get hold of. If something felt good, they did it. Even when it didn't feel so good any more, they kept on doing it. Jimmy's standard had always been simple: if he could get up on stage the next night and play, he was doing all right. Since he always answered the bell, he fooled himself into believing he didn't have a problem.

Jimmy's roundabout road to sobriety had begun ten years earlier in Pocatello, Idaho.

Chapter Two

The Black Velvets were playing a good-sized roadhouse bar called Aces and Deuces, just outside Pocatello near the intersection of Idaho Highway 91 with the interstate. The *Urban Cowboy* craze had passed years before, but the Aces still had a mechanical bull sitting in one corner covered with an old tarp. It was a good gig by Jimmy's standards, Wednesday through Saturday. The Magic Bus smelled a lot better when it stayed in one place long enough to get laundry done.

Wednesday night was Ladies' Night. That meant $1.50 well drinks and no cover charge for women, a proven method of attracting men by association. It was working that night: the bar and dance floor were packed. The Black Velvets were in the middle of their first set, wrapping up their version of *Sympathy for the Devil,* when Jimmy spotted a cute blonde dancing in front of the stage. She had a pixie haircut, tight jeans, laughing eyes and dimples for days. He played the game he so often played, smiling and seeming to direct his solos to her alone. When the Velvets took their twenty-minute break, Jimmy wandered through the crowd to the bar.

"Seven and seven," said Jimmy to the bartender. Sure enough, he felt a soft touch on his shoulder. He turned and met the merry eyes. *It's so easy, it should be illegal*. Jimmy smiled and raised his eyebrows.

"Hi. I'm Debbie." She somehow managed to be both shy and flirtatious at the same time. Jimmy was smitten, a frequent and short-lived reaction in his world.

"I'm Jimmy," he said, as if his name were not all over the reader board outside, the bass drum and a large roll-up sign at the back of the stage.

"I know. I…I just wanted to tell you…you guys are so great. I don't know why you're playing here. You should be playing somewhere good."

Jimmy agreed, but didn't like hearing it from a girl he was hitting on. His smile faltered a bit.

"Thanks," he said. "We won't be playing these kinds of places much longer. We've been talking to a rep from one of the big labels and it's looking good. We're only playing here because we were already booked."

He had told this lie so often, he almost believed it himself.

"When you're famous, I'll tell people I met you at the Aces and Deuces and they'll never believe me."

"Hey," Jimmy said, as if the idea had just occurred to him, "we're having a little after-show party tonight. It'll just be the band and a few of our friends. Do you want to come?"

She looked doubtful. "I don't think so," she said. "I'm not a 'party with the band' kind of girl. I'm sure it would be fun, but I really shouldn't be here at all–I've got two finals staring me in the face on Friday."

"Oh, are you a student?"

She nodded. "Idaho State. I'll be graduating in a couple of months."

There was a brief and uncomfortable pause. "Good for you," Jimmy said. "Well, I've gotta get back on stage. Hang around after the show if you change your mind." Jimmy reached out and squeezed her arm before weaving his way through the crowd around the bar.

The Black Velvets kicked off the next set with *It's a Long Way to the Top (If You Wanna Rock 'n Roll).* He scanned the crowd for Debbie during his guitar solo, but she was nowhere in sight. By the time the last note echoed off the back of the bar, he knew he'd struck out. *Easy come, easy go.* Another girl appeared at the front of the stage, and he took her to the 'after party' back at the Motel Six.

He didn't see Debbie on Thursday or Friday night, either. Few women lingered in Jimmy's memory after they were out of sight, but Debbie did. Even as other attractive girls showed up in front of the stage, trying to catch his eye, his thoughts kept returning to her.

Midway through the second set on Saturday night, he spotted Debbie again. She was dancing with a young guy in a cowboy hat, but she glanced up and flashed Jimmy a quick smile.

After a few more songs, Jimmy stepped to the microphone and said, "Don't go anywhere, The Black Velvets will be right back." He set his Strat down in its stand, jumped down from the stage, and walked straight over to the table where Debbie was sitting with a pretty brunette and a bookish-looking redhead.

"Well, if it isn't Debbie from Idaho State. How you doin'?"

She smiled at him. Somewhere inside, Jimmy felt his façade tremble a bit.

"I'm good. I didn't think you'd remember me. These are my friends Janet and Emily," she said, nodding to her friends. The names passed by without Jimmy noticing.

"Pleased to meet you. So, Debbie, how'd those finals go?"

Her smile widened. "I won't know until next week, but there's nothing else I can do about it now, so we came out to blow off a little steam and hear some good music."

"That's why we're here. We've got one more set to go, then we're off tomorrow. I think the band's gonna have a little get-together after the bar closes, though. You want to come?"

Debbie glanced at her friends, but shook her head a little. "No, I don't think so, but thank you."

Man, this gal is tough to get through to. He gave her his most hangdog, lopsided grin and said, "I'll tell you what. I can never crash right after we're done playing. I'm too wound up. There's a Denny's down the street. Why don't you come pick me up here and I'll buy you breakfast."

She hesitated. *Close the deal.* "I've gotta do this last set and tear down our equipment, but I'll be ready to go about 2:30. Come pick me up then, okay?" Before she could answer, Jimmy was back onstage, launching into the intro of *Welcome to the*

Jungle. Two songs later, Jimmy played Buddy Holly's *True Love Ways* and looked Debbie in the eye the entire song.

That keys into even the stickiest locks.

Before closing time, Debbie and her friends left the club, but she glanced back before she reached the door. Jimmy smiled and nodded at her.

Ninety minutes later, when Jimmy walked out the back door of the Aces and Deuces, a silver Honda Accord idled in the parking lot with Debbie behind the wheel.

"Hello, Sunshine," Jimmy said, opening the passenger door and sliding in. "Who's for breakfast?"

"I'm pretty sure you mean *what's* for breakfast, don't you?"

"Who, what, let's not quibble over details. I'm starved. A couple of handfuls of peanuts at the bar did not hold me through three long sets of rock 'n roll. Let's go!"

The Denny's parking lot was still half full when they pulled in at 3 AM. A waitress poured coffee into thick ceramic mugs. Debbie said, "I'm sure you meet girls at every town you play in…"

"Not every town," Jimmy interrupted. *Because I always strike out in Yakima, for some reason. Considering Yakima, that might be for the best.*

"…but I'm not going to be anyone's 'Pocatello girl.' I admit I'm flattered you picked me out of the crowd on Wednesday, but I'm just here to have breakfast with you. Tomorrow, you'll be on down the road to…"

"Lewiston. We're playing in Lewiston next."

"…right, you'll be on the road to Lewiston. And I'll be here, in college, having gone back to my apartment to sleep in my own bed, by myself."

"That's not what..." Her look said: *I am not an idiot.* He smiled a little and said, "Okay. No worries. I promised I'd buy you breakfast though, so order up."

By the time their Grand Slams had arrived, Debbie had told most of her story. She grew up in nearby Chubbuck; her dad was a mortgage lending manager at Idaho Central Credit Union. In two more quarters, she would get her degree. Through all four years of college, she'd lived like a nun. She liked dancing and music, but not enough to make her careless. *I guess I was still sort of hoping to get lucky. That isn't going to happen. And you know what? I don't care. This was all right anyway, score or no score.*

By the time they left Denny's, the Eastern sky was turning pink. Debbie drove Jimmy to the Motel Six and let him off right beside the Magic Bus. Before he got out, Jimmy reached across the seat and kissed her. "Thanks for an unexpected night."

She handed him a slip of paper. "Here's my number. If you want to call me, you can, but I won't hold my breath. Goodnight and goodbye, Jimmy Velvet."

Jimmy smiled and said "I'll call you."

"Maybe you will," she said, in a tone that said *Nah, you won't.*

The gig in Lewiston came and went, followed by more one-night stands and weekenders in small towns around the Pacific Northwest. A few weeks went by, including a few more after-party hookups, but none of the girls stuck in his mind. Finally, one cold blowy afternoon in Moses Lake, while Rollie was fueling up the bus, Jimmy slunk over to a payphone. He dropped in four quarters and dialed the number on the slip of paper he'd been carrying in his pocket since that morning at the Motel Six.

After three distant rings, he heard her voice. "Hello?"

"Debbie, it's Jimmy."

"Well, surprise, surprise. Who's for breakfast today, Jimmy Velvet?"

Over the next few weeks, the calls became a habit. He called her from payphones all over Washington, Oregon and Idaho. While Jimmy never seemed to have enough quarters to talk for very long, he developed the habit of checking in with her once or twice a week. If her answering machine came on, he would often sing a few bars of *True Love Ways*.

Months passed, and bitter winter turned to soggy spring in Idaho. Debbie survived another round of finals, graduating with honors. Four years of mental and emotional discipline had paid off, leaving her drained but successful. Her quiet life suddenly felt much too quiet. To the chagrin of her disapproving parents and roommates, she took off to meet Jimmy, telling herself she wouldn't be gone long.

From the moment she caught up with Jimmy in Longview, Washington, they were a couple. She didn't love life on the road as the guitarist's girlfriend, so she picked out a little one-bedroom apartment outside Portland. It didn't matter where it was on the bar circuit, because Jimmy spent such long stretches on the road. She soon found work as a receptionist at a construction company. The job was fine, but she lived for the times when Jimmy was home. It wasn't a perfect arrangement, but she made it work. By autumn, she began to realize she was falling in love with Jimmy.

Over the next eighteen months, Jimmy and Debbie were together as much as they could be. When he wasn't touring, he crashed at Debbie's apartment. They even started calling it "our place." Jimmy never made much money, though, and her receptionist job wasn't enough to support both of them. They would have a few weeks together, and soon Jimmy would be off for another tour of the same familiar joints in hot spots like Prineville, Oregon and Othello, Washington.

Debbie started living a double life. Most of the time, she was the quiet young working woman she had planned to be. When Jimmy was around, she became a rock 'n roll hanger-on. Until she'd met him, she had been a light drinker. When it came to drinking, Jimmy was a pro, but Debbie caught on fast. She was small, but it turned out she could hold her booze. Soon she was holding way too much, too much of the time. After a while, she didn't even wait for the excuse of having Jimmy around.

When it reached the stage at which she was tempted to sneak vodka to her work, Debbie saw the road she was heading down. *This is not what I want out of life*. Unlike everyone else that was in the band's orbit—some of whom had, now and then, confessed similar thoughts to her—Debbie did something about it. While Jimmy was on one of his epic month-long tours of glamor venues like Madras, Hermiston, La Grande, and Baker City, Oregon, she dried out and got her head straight. She started going to AA meetings, got a sponsor she could call day or night, and began working the Twelve Steps. The message took.

When Jimmy got back to their tiny studio apartment, he found her sitting on their ratty couch, looking tired, thin, and beautiful. He had never noticed the damage she had inflicted on herself by drinking too much, but he saw the struggle on her face. It hurt him. She patted the cushion beside her.

"C'mere, Jimmy. We've gotta talk."

No good conversation ever starts with those words.

Jimmy smiled at her and obeyed.

"I can't do this anymore," she said. "It was killing me, or at least killing a part of me. I like that part, and I'm not willing to let her go. I've got to get off this merry-go-round and find my real life again."

"C'mon, baby," Jimmy said. "There's nothing wrong with a little ride on the merry-go-round." He grinned and tried to pull her closer, but she pushed him away.

"There is for me, Jimmy. I can't do it. I can't wait around any more for you to grow up."

Since she was twenty-three and he was thirty-four, that stung him a little bit. "Okay, baby, I get it. You know I love you and I'll do anything for you. If that means I need to quit drinking and everything else, I will. I promise."

He had meant it, sort of. What he really meant was, "I'll quit drinking and everything else *while I'm around you.* The rest of the time, what does it hurt if I have a good time?"

And so it was. At home, Jimmy walked the straight and narrow. As soon as he got back on the bus, he slipped back into his old habits, as comfortable as his favorite pair of Levis. All seemed right with his world.

Most heavy drinkers have great capacity for self-delusion, and that included Jimmy. Debbie, however, didn't blind herself.

When he returned from another long road trip, her car was not in the driveway. The lock made a strangely empty sound as he keyed into the house. He entered to find a cold apartment, emptied of everything she owned. She had left him the couch and a note.

> *I'm sorry. I love you. I told you I couldn't do this anymore.*

Oddly, the apartment felt so much smaller with her stuff gone.

What bothered Jimmy most is that he wanted to feel something. *I'm supposed to feel something, damn it.* The only thing he did feel, though, was that he needed a drink.

I think I've found the problem, and it is me.

On that road trip, Jimmy had lost his bassist and rhythm guitarist to another band, so The Black Velvets were in dry dock for a while. That gave him a surplus of time to think about life. He had no idea where Debbie was. He tried calling her friends and family in Idaho, but most wouldn't talk to him. Those who would take his calls seemed pleased enough to tell him that they hadn't seen her, and didn't know where she was.

When Jimmy realized Debbie was gone for good, it sobered him up in more than one way. *Maybe*, he thought, *this is the growing up she was waiting for. Maybe I just had one too many bouts of the brown bottle flu.* Whatever the cause, while Rollie rebuilt The Black Velvets into incarnation number eleven, Jimmy went off to rehab.

He'd been sober ever since.

Three months later, he got a letter with no return address. When he opened it, a single piece of stationary fell out.

> *I'm pregnant. I don't need anything from you. I just wanted you to know.*
>
> *--Debbie*

Chapter Three

Above the driver's seat in the Magic Bus was a series of pictures of a little girl. From left to right, she got older. It began with wallet-sized baby pictures of her against holiday backgrounds. At two, she was dragging a stuffed brown bunny by the ears. Then she was sitting proudly astride a teeter-totter, showing off her missing front teeth. By second grade, she was wearing a too-big Black Velvets T-shirt. Debbie had told him she had insisted on wearing it for school pictures. On the far right was her third grade picture, showing a pretty, pigtailed, serious-looking girl. When Jimmy had called to ask why she looked so somber, she'd said, "I couldn't find my smile that day, but they took the picture anyway."

Jimmy wasn't in any of the pictures.

Rollie looked up at the overhead mirror, saw Jimmy staring at the photos. "Missing Emily, Jim? We should be able to take a few weeks off after the Valentine's Day show in Spokane. Maybe you can get over to Pocatello then."

"Maybe. That would be good. She's been on my mind a lot."

Rollie raised his bushy eyebrows. "Just Emily, or Emily and Debbie?"

Jimmy fixed the mirror image with a warning look. "I haven't talked to Debbie about anything other than Emily for five years. I think she's dating a dentist now. A freaking dentist." Jimmy turned his face to the darkness outside the window.

The Magic Bus gave a little shudder as Rollie shifted gears and they hit the dip between the Eagles Nest parking lot and the highway. After so many wee-hours journeys, Rollie and Jimmy had long since reached an understanding about getting back on the road. Rollie always drove the first shift, and Jimmy sat in the first seat and stayed awake to talk to him.

The Magic Bus was set up for long hauls. A mini-refrigerator and microwave sat behind the driver's seat, along with a small television hooked up to a VCR. The younger Velvets spent their time between gigs watching Bruce Willis and Arnold Schwarzenegger movies. When Jimmy took control of the VCR, he watched the dozens of bootleg concert videos he had collected over the years. When he and Rollie had first started the band, all he cared about was looking good and meeting girls. Over time, that changed. The music became its own calling, and he took what he could from each of the legendary performers he had on tape.

As they rolled down the road late at night, Jimmy would often put on a video of Otis Redding or Humble Pie or Janis Joplin and let them provide the soundtrack for the drive. Tonight, he was too tired to do anything but watch the darkened miles blend together. They'd been on the road for several hours and the sun was just beginning to lighten the eastern sky. They rode in companionable silence, listening to the familiar squeaks and groans of the old bus, when one of the squeaks became a squeal.

The shrill alarm of the noise jerked Jimmy from his reverie and he glanced outside to see where they were. The terrain was very familiar: near the top of the Lashton Grade, heading down toward the river. The squeal grew louder. An unnerving shimmy ran through the front of the bus.

"Hey, Jim. You awake?" Rollie's voice, dead calm.

"You know I am, brother. What's going on with the bus?"

At that moment, the squeal stopped. The noise had been bad, but the sudden silence was worse—the moment in a horror movie just before the killer jumps out from behind the door.

"I don't want to spook you, man, but I think our brakes just went out. All the way out. I've got the pedal jammed all the way to the floor, but we're pickin' up speed. " Rollie said. "We've got a long downhill grade ahead of us and I'm having trouble slowin' this girl down."

If there had been a note of panic in Rollie's voice, Jimmy might have thought he was joking around. The calm flatness told him they were in honest-to-god trouble.

"Oh, shit. Okay, okay, let's not panic. We've been down this road a million times. It's a pretty long straight stretch ahead, right?"

"Right," Rollie said. "The switchbacks are behind us, but there's the big turn to the left just before we get to the river. If we hit that doin' more than about 45, we're screwed."

"How fast are we going right now?"

"We're up to about 75."

Jimmy was wide awake now. Adrenaline pumped through him, and the faster the railing zipped by, the more time slowed.

Rollie was hauling on the gear shift, trying to downshift. That was a bitch under normal circumstances, much more so while hurtling down the side of a mountain at this speed. *He will never get that done with one arm, and he has to steer.* Jimmy leaped forward, throwing his weight against the stick along with Rollie's hand. Just when he thought it was a lost cause, the lower gear engaged and a shudder ran through the whole bus. The rear end swung sharply to the right, far enough to alert everyone with the grinding screech of metal scraping metal as the bus left paint on the guard rail. Rollie overcorrected, sending them fishtailing close to the edge of the oncoming lane, but muscled the Magic Bus back into their proper lane.

As variations of "what the hell, man" issued from the back of the bus, Jimmy looked over Rollie's shoulder at the speedometer. 65 MPH and dropping. The transmission was screaming in protest, but Jimmy knew they would have to jam it down at least one more gear to have any shot at making the corner up ahead. He looked up to see how much time they had left.

They were out of time.

Rollie let out a guttural, wordless yell and jammed the steering wheel hard to the left.

It wasn't even close.

Just before the crucial turn, the road hit its low point and sloped slightly upward, shaving a couple of miles per hour of their speed. Not enough. The Magic Bus blew through the right-side guardrail at sixty miles an hour. Time slowed again, and the bus flew free in space for one insane moment, then canted nose downward.

At this bend, the Lashton River was shallow and white-watery nearest the road, deeper on the far side. Jimmy's stomach flipped over as the bus hurtled toward the deep part. Jimmy cut loose with an intellectual revelation: "OH SHIT!" There wasn't time for much more.

The Magic Bus struck the river, front tires and bumper first, at a vertical angle of roughly 30°. Upon impact, it was leaning and turned slightly to the right. As the water arrested the bus's velocity, every loose item in it flew forward, slightly upward and to the right: amplifiers, suitcases, beer bottles, pizza boxes, human beings and more flew around in pandemonium. As the current pressed against the underside of the bus, the vehicle rolled slowly onto its side, then onto its roof and began to settle.

Darkness.

The initial impact had tossed Jimmy against the roof. He lay against it, half buried under everything that constituted a rock 'n roll life on the road.

The impact had knocked everyone out to some degree, but not for long. Water rushed in through the bus's damaged front door, its chill shocking Jimmy back to consciousness in a hurry. The only light was the headlights, pointing out into the darkness of the river at a crazy angle.

Jimmy tried to stand amid the debris. His head throbbed. When he touched his forehead, his hand came away sticky. There was an unpleasant taste in his mouth, as if he had broken some teeth. He was dizzy and wanted to throw up, but the bus was filling up with river water fast. It was already past his knees.

Rollie had been thrown first against the windshield, spider webbing the old glass without shattering it, then sliding down toward the door in a heap. The water was stirring up a bit of consciousness in him as well, but not quite enough. Jimmy grabbed him by the shoulder and shook him hard, screaming full throat. "Rollie! Come on, man, don't leave me now. I'm gonna go check on the guys in the back, make sure they're okay, so we can all get out. C'mon now, sit up!"

Jimmy could see movement around the middle of the bus: Drew and Mark, whose flight had evidently terminated against the backs of the three remaining rows of old seats. His first impulse was to remind them of the emergency exits. *Why do you think this bus is obsolete for kids, dumbass? They didn't have any emergency exits back in 1959!* To Jimmy's relief, both began working their way toward the front. Jimmy crawled up toward them. "What the hell?" asked Drew, groggily.

"Rollie's halfway knocked out up front. I'm gonna go make sure J.J.'s all right, then we'll be right behind you. Try and get the crap out of the way so you can open the front door. We'll be right behind you!"

They both nodded and headed to the front of the bus, where Rollie was sort of floating alongside an empty KFC bucket. After a few minutes, Jimmy heard a sploosh as they wrenched the front door open. Water gushed in, though for the moment the Magic Bus didn't seem to be sinking. *Must be the trapped air.* When he finally got to the back of the bus, J.J. was unconscious and bleeding badly from the head. Jimmy dragged him through all the floating crap and underwater crap, hauled him under the water, then shoved him out the front doorway. Jimmy hit his head on the back of the driver's seat on his way up for air, a minor discomfort in a flood of great discomforts.

He remembered Rollie, but his old friend was gone—where, he didn't know. Jimmy took a dive in the front to hunt for Rollie; no luck. The bus was shifting more as the doorway caught the river's flow. *Wherever he is, he's not trapped in here. I can get the hell out of here now.*

He turned toward the front of the bus, fighting the rushing river water. He pushed his face against what had been the bus's floor and took three rapid breaths, filling his lungs with as much oxygen as he could. It took desperate strength, but Jimmy managed to swim against the current and out through the front door.

As he did so, one of Emily's pictures floated near enough past his face that he managed to spot it in what little moonlight penetrated the water. It was the one where she had been unable to find her smile. He grasped for it, kicking to try and reach the surface, but an eddy in the current hindered his desperate efforts. The air in his lungs was coming out whether he wanted it to or not, and when it did, in rushed a torrent of icy water. Jimmy panicked, thrashing with the last of his strength as if effort alone could launch him toward air.

There was nothing but darkness and water everywhere, and his vision dimmed. The last thing he saw was the picture of Emily, one more time, swirling around in the little maelstrom created by his struggles. He tried to reach for it, but his fingers wouldn't respond.

Calm washed over Jimmy. He closed his eyes and let go of life.

Chapter Four

Jimmy Velvet opened his eyes.

He was still underwater, but the bus and floating debris from the crash were gone. The water had gone from icy cold to body-temperature warm, and felt thicker than it should have. Somewhere above him, a light shimmered.

He was in over his head, but he felt no need to breathe. He kicked easily toward the light, moving faster than he expected. When his head broke the surface, he was somewhere different than where the bus had broken through the rail. He didn't know where he was, but he wasn't at the bottom of the Lashton grade any more. It wasn't dark, it wasn't cold, and nothing ached or stung.

Stuck underwater, can't breathe, now everything around me has changed...son of a bitch, I can figure out what that means.

Jimmy crawled onto a shore where both the beach and the water stretched unbroken as far as he could see. He collapsed on his back and tried to get his bearings. He saw no sun, just light diffused throughout the sky without an identifiable source. The horizon reached upward in all directions, forming a sepia-toned, opaque nothingness.

It's like something sucked all the color out of everything.

He looked down and even his Ramones t-shirt, blue jeans and Chuck Taylors seemed subdued and colorless.

I can't believe I'm dead, but I guess it doesn't matter if I believe it or not.

Jimmy stood and looked around, but saw only unbroken landscape.

Emily.

Emily's face rose unbidden in his memory. Small flashes of her followed, laughing, crying, looking up at him, saying, "I love you, Daddy."

I'll never see her again, hold her, love her. Shit. I was a crappy dad. I always believed there was time. Emily, I'm sorry...

Maybe it's time to quit bullshitting myself. I never would have changed. I would have stayed on the road, playing dives for nickels and dimes until I was too old to pick up my Strat.

Jimmy held his head in his hands, thinking of the people he had loved and left behind. He sat there long enough for his clothes to dry out, yet the sky didn't change color. There was no sound. He clapped his hands, but it sounded muffled. His environment seemed indifferent to anything he did.

Ever since he was a young man, Jimmy had said that when he died, he wanted to go to Hell, because that's where all his friends would be. Confronted with the possibility of getting his wish, that didn't seem so funny anymore. A lot of his natural cockiness drained away. He knew he hadn't lived a perfect life—far from it—but he had always believed *the man upstairs will understand.*

In life, Jimmy had heard stories about tunnels and bright lights and dead relatives waiting for you when you died, but all he saw here was an unrelenting drabness. *I have no idea what I should be doing; I guess I could just sit here and think. My watch is gone. There's no sun. No hunger, no thirst, no sleepiness. If there's supposed to be a welcoming committee here for me, somebody screwed it up. I guess I'll walk and see if I can find somebody. Anybody.*

Jimmy stood up. There was something strange about that. What was it? *Yes. It didn't hurt. No groaning, no pushing off the ground, no aching back. It's like when I was young. Well, a swim in that weird, thick water doesn't sound very appealing right now, so I'll just walk.* After just a few steps, he turned and looked at the way he had come. The water was gone.

I'll be damned.

Shit. I shouldn't say that either! At least I didn't put 'God' in front of 'damned.' Maybe now is not the time to take His name in vain. Death changes your perspective.

With no landmarks, Jimmy shrugged his shoulders and set off, whistling *You Can't Always Get What You Want*. He saw a structure of some sort in the distance, which eventually came into focus as a roughly hewn bridge...over nothing but more sand. Whatever was on the other side of the bridge was lost in a swirl of mist and lights.

Maybe I got dropped off in the wrong place, and this is where Dad and Grandma and everyone are supposed to meet me. I don't know if anyone will be particularly glad to see me. Do they make mistakes in Heaven? That sounds more like something you'd expect in Hell. Maybe there's a Purgatory that's nothing but a steady stream of screw-ups, like the DMV.

Jimmy laid his hand on the bridge and peered across, trying to make out what was on the other side. *It would be logical to walk across and find out, but that might not be a good idea. I can take some time to think about this. If whatever's over there really wants to see me, they can send a squadron of angels looking for me. Or demons. It could go either way, really.*

The tune to Jimmy Cliff's *Sitting in Limbo* came into his head, so Jimmy sat on the edge of the bridge and sang all the verses he could remember, then sang them again. Nobody showed up.

He eventually got tired of waiting. *Might as well head across.* Jimmy put a foot up on the bridge and put his weight on it, testing for stability, then laughed at himself. *What's it gonna do, kill me?*

Without a trace of irony, he said "What the hell," and crossed the bridge. Nothing happened. He stepped carefully off the far side onto the sand, but there were no trumpets, no Voice of God, no whiff of brimstone.

He took a few steps away, then looked over his shoulder. He wasn't surprised to see that the bridge had vanished. It didn't take long for the miraculous and impossible to become ordinary and disappearing objects seemed to become mundane.

The far side of the bridge appeared to be exactly like the side he had come from, but when he looked up, the sky had opened and he saw a faint golden light emanating from some impossible distance. Jimmy shaded his eyes with his hand and tried to focus on the golden light.

As he did, he was lifted bodily upward toward the light.

Just like the sixties, man.

He strained his neck up to stare at the light, then tried going spread-eagle. His positioning and contortions did nothing to alter his ascent toward the light. At first, it was kind of cool—like having one of those dreams of flying, except he didn't wake up. Nor did he arrive at the light any time soon. After what felt like a few hours the novelty wore off, and Jimmy found himself once again alone with his thoughts.

Jimmy had never been very introspective, but he now found some comfort in having time to let his mind catch up with everything. He had heard that when you died, your whole life flashed before your eyes. All he had seen as he crossed over was the photo of Emily floating out of his reach.

Emily.

Thoughts of her followed him as he ascended.

Tears ran down his face.

And now, here's Jimmy Velvet's hot new single: Tears of Shame.

What a joke. I had to die to figure out what was important in life.

Isn't that taking stubborn to its ultimate meaning?

He looked up. The sun, or whatever was making that light, was still a universe away.

Thinking about Emily is getting me nowhere. She's got Debbie. She's always been both mom and dad to her, so that'll be okay. She'll be okay. She has to be. I can't do anything for her now. My heart's empty. He didn't need to breathe, but he found he could still sigh. As he continued to rise, his mind wandered over the course of his life.

He remembered his tenth birthday, when Uncle Bill had given him his first guitar. He had unwrapped a gift from his parents that he had hoped was a BB gun, but it was just a cap gun. In response to his disappointed eyes, his mom had said: “We thought you weren’t quite ready for the responsibility of a BB gun. Maybe next year.” *Considering the way my life turned out, I can't fault her.*

His disappointment hadn’t lasted long. Uncle Bill had said, “Never mind about shooting things, I’ve got something better.” He had run out to his old pickup parked in the driveway and returned with Jimmy’s first guitar. It wasn’t a dime store toy, but a used Epiphone archtop—a big guitar for a little boy. Scuffs and marks showed here and there on its surface.

I bet my jaw hung down to my jeans.

Uncle Bill said: “This was my first guitar. My uncle gave it to me when I was just a little older than you, and now I’m giving it to you. This is a real guitar, not a toy, so you need to treat it with the respect it deserves, or I’ll take it back. Owning a guitar is a responsibility. Let’s see if you’re ready for that.” He glanced at his sister-in-law, but didn’t say anything to her.

She was a little pissed, but that was all right. When you're ten, your mom disapproves of everything that's cool. Anyway, she disapproved of everything Uncle Bill did, or maybe what he didn't do. His uncle either hadn't noticed, or hadn't cared, because he knelt in front of Jimmy and slipped the guitar strap around his neck for the first time.

It was a moment that set the course of his life.

Mom always thought Uncle Bill should settle down, become respectable, find a real job, get married, have some kids. She probably blamed him for the direction I took, and I can see why. Uncle Bill lived an itinerant life, traveling from town to town, playing guitar and singing in pick-up bands in honky-tonks all over America. *Gee, what did I end up doing? But I couldn't help it. That first time I strummed a chord, I was home. Even though I couldn't quite get my hands around the neck, by the end of that birthday I was almost playing* I’m So

Lonesome I Could Cry. *If Mom had been a lyricist, she might have composed her own version,* I'm So Annoyed I Could Break Things. *Uncle Bill was such a patient teacher. I was thirty before I figured out why: the music was part of his soul.*

That tenth birthday shone bittersweet in his memory: the first time he held a guitar, but the last time he saw Uncle Bill. Just a few months later, Bill Andrzejewski died in a car accident on the way to Biloxi, Mississippi.

That set off a stream of memories.

The summer he was thirteen, he and his friends discovered a road a couple of miles from his house that went up and down two hills like a rollercoaster. They spent much of that summer riding down the first hill at breakneck speed, laughing like crazy and pedaling as fast as they could up and over the other one. *I can still feel that anticipation, my stomach dropping, when I hit the top of the second hill going balls out. We couldn't see what was coming until that last moment. And then we turned around and did it again. And again, and again.*

That was a great time.

Jimmy thought back to bucking bales in the hayfields outside Tenino the summer he was fifteen. Stripped to the waist, walking alongside the truck under the beating sun, throwing hay bales up higher and higher to the guy stacking them. *I sweated so much, so much pollen and hay dust stuck to me, I looked even browner than my tan.* Those first few mornings, he was so sore he needed help from his mom to get out of bed the next morning, but he got used to it. "Toughened you up a little bit," his dad had said. Years later, his dad would say, "That summer was probably the only honest work you ever did."

Can't disagree.

He'd spent the rest of that summer at his grandparents' house near Moses Lake, in eastern Washington. *Thanks to bucking hay, I was in the best shape of my life. I was a stud, full of piss and vinegar.* The days had belonged to his Gramps, who was old enough to need help around his place, but at night Jimmy snuck out of the house and hitchhiked into town just to see what could be seen. He was tall for his age, able to pass for eighteen or nineteen in spite of his inability to grow any sort of beard.

The second night out, Jimmy hit pay dirt in the form of a bar called Lumpy’s, where they weren’t too stuffy about checking ID. *I have to give Lumpy's credit for some milestones in my life: my first drink, my first hangover, and especially my first glimpse of real, live rock ‘n roll.* His first drink was a whiskey, because that was the only drink he could think of. His first hangover arrived right on schedule the next morning, but he managed to convince his Gran that it was a summer flu bug. *Or so I thought. I wouldn't be able to fool myself now; do I really think I fooled her? Doubt it. But that was the night I met the only drug I could never kick: rock ‘n roll.*

The band was set up on a small stage in a corner. The patrons paid them no attention as they set up their instruments and said “Check. Check. Check, one, two,” into their microphones. The long-haired guitarist stepped to the microphone and said, “I’m Happy Harold, and these are the Howlers. This is an old song, but we just heard a new version of it that we like. We don’t know it by heart yet, but we’ll figure it out as we go along.” The opening chords of *Summertime Blues* drowned out all conversation. The band didn't cover the 1950s Eddie Cochran version, but instead launched the full-on aural assault of Blue Cheer's recently released version. The lead guitarist blitzed out huge, chunky power chords while the drummer, his blonde hair falling over his face like a curtain, bashed away at his drums like they owed him money. The bass player stood stock still, only his fingers moving as they flew over the frets.

The sound entered through Jimmy’s ears, passed through his brain and went straight to his soul. He took it with him to a watery grave.

Happy Harold was right; they didn’t have it down cold, but it didn’t matter. A minute into the song, the dance floor was packed.

Jimmy spent the rest of his vacation sneaking out every night, trying not to stand out lest he attract notice and get thrown out. He watched the Howlers thrash on their instruments, and did not fail to notice how the girls in the bar stared at the band when their boyfriends weren't paying attention.

The birth was still some time away, but Jimmy 'Guitar' Velvet was conceived that summer at Lumpy's.

Jimmy looked up at the sky above. The golden light was brighter now, but still far off. He let his mind drift back to the fall of 1970. Fifteen months out of high school, his parents were trying to push him out of the nest, but The Black Velvets weren't a full-time gig yet. Helping people find the right size bolts at the local hardware store or delivering their pizza did not appeal to him. He had been letting his hair grow long for years, but long hair and flower power hadn't reached Jimmy's home town. Hair past his shoulders marked Jimmy as "one of those damn hippies."

In September, Jimi Hendrix died. The news hit harder in Washington, Jimi's home state, and a strange thing happened. People he didn't know, and who normally wouldn't give him the time of day, went out of their way to talk and commiserate with him, as if Jimmy's long hair and funky clothes somehow made him a long-lost relative of Jimi's.

A month later, Janis Joplin died. Jimmy took that news even harder. When he listened to her heartbroken blues shouts, the thought of that rough, piercing voice silenced forever felt like a personal loss. The same thing happened: random locals offered him their sympathies. *That's when the train wreck started, too. I always said: live fast, die young, and leave a good-looking corpse. My life philosophy was fixed by their deaths, people I idolized but hadn't ever met.*

Guess I didn't live out my philosophy. One out of three, and even the living fast part, I eased up in my thirties.

Shortly thereafter, Jimmy formed the first full-fledged version of what would become The Black Velvets. Jimmy handled most of the vocals and played lead guitar, joined by "Stormin'" Norman Pompeo on drums, Jon Averill on bass and the unforgettable Hezekiah "Smitty" Smith on rhythm guitar. *Ha! No wonder he didn't answer to his real name. Sounded Amish or something. We stopped kidding him about churning butter, and calling him 'thou,' after it got old within a month.*

That incarnation of the band lasted nearly four years, bringing Jimmy as close as he ever got to his dreams of stardom. In late 1973, Jimmy and Jon sat down after a show and wrote a song called *Rock 'n Roll Boogaloo.* It wasn't much on lyrics—"Oh won't you, won't you do/The Rock 'n Roll Boogaloo/With me"—made up most of the chorus, but it got a great reaction at their live shows. Guys in suits started showing up, record reps. A record deal seemed just around the corner. The Velvets scraped together enough money to hire a studio and laid down a great party version of the song. They believed they were on their way.

Not quite.

As the labels' interest peaked, Rick Derringer released *Rock 'n Roll Hootchie Coo.* That song became a monster hit. The Black Velvets and *Rock 'n Roll Boogaloo* looked like wannabes trying to cash in on somebody else's hit. The door of opportunity slammed shut. The guys in the suits stopped coming around. Stormin' Norman and Smitty soon parted ways with the Black Velvets, and Jimmy was strapped in for his first real ride on the rock 'n roll rollercoaster.

As he continued to rise toward the light, Jimmy's mind wandered over the many versions of the band. *I can't even remember half the names or faces offhand. Most of them bagged out on us. Jon Averill, he's one who didn't skip, but he was our worst loss.* In 1977, while the steady rhythm of disco ruled the charts and The Black Velvets were on one of their endless tours, Jon overdosed and died in the bathroom of a crappy motel in Walla Walla. *Some people dismiss bass players and drummers as "the rhythm section," as if their roles don't matter, but if a band loses either one of them, it's probably going to fall apart.*

That's how it was for us. When Jon ODed, something died that we never got back.

Jon's death should have been a warning to Jimmy, but he went the other direction. If death was inevitable anyway, why not meet it head on in a Corvette doing 100 miles an hour? Jimmy started to drink more and more, and expanded his horizons as to what acceptable drug use meant. It took a toll. *Between then and my late thirties, shit, I can't remember a lot. Parties I remember. People I remember. Which people were at which parties, don't ask me.*

Mamas, don't let your babies grow up to be rockers.

Jimmy remembered the time that Rollie had gotten in a fight with a big biker at a dive called Baldy's. *The guy was a grizzly bear. He took a big swing at Rollie, and my man didn't duck fast enough. It knocked him ass-backwards into the center stage microphone. What the hell was I singing? Yeah,* Dirty Deeds Done Dirt Cheap. *I ate the mic, broke two of my teeth. It ended with Rollie and the biker hugging each other like old buds. I thought about telling them to book a room, and having the good sense to not say that was probably one of the few good decisions I made in those days. Took me forever to get my teeth fixed.*

Good times, good times.

Jimmy drifted off to some form of sleep, then awoke. *The light is a lot closer now, so I must have crashed for quite a while.* Now the sky was softer, with blue tones rather than brown, and wisps of cloud going past as he ascended.

It was starting to look like the way Jimmy had imagined Heaven, back when he had gone to church with his mom. Every Sunday, he started with good intentions, trying his best to listen to the minister. Then his mind would start to drift, he'd end up daydreaming, and by the time it was over he rarely had any idea what the sermon had been about. *I did try to focus on stuff that wouldn't offend God, since He probably paid more attention to me in church. As I remember, I spent most of my time wondering what was so great about Heaven that it would be worth passing up the sins and temptations the preacher kept warning us against.*

Jimmy craned his neck around, checking to see if there were any little angels sitting on the cloud puffs. *Would I be seeing something different if I was born somewhere else, or some*when *else? Does Heaven conform to whatever I was taught to expect, or do my own beliefs form what I am seeing?*

No idea. What I can see, though, is that I'm getting closer to that light.

It had started as more of an indistinct impression than an actual light. It now took up his whole field of vision. *Like I’m being pulled directly into the sun. But it isn't burning my skin. Kind of feels like it's burning something out of me from the inside, even healing me. I'm tripping, but this is better than any drug I ever took. I'd have never gone to rehab if I could have gotten stash like this.* He gave himself over to the light, letting it cleanse every corner of his being.

At that exact moment, whatever invisible elevator had been carrying him upward came to a sudden halt. Solid ground formed beneath Jimmy’s feet: he stood on warm, fragrant grass. *This has to be the kind of grass John Sebastian was laying on when he wrote* Daydream.

The golden light spread out in every direction, filling the sky. Out in the distance, Jimmy saw rolling green hills dotted with small clusters of wildflowers. *I think I even hear a little creek somewhere, bubbling along. It's like a meadow on the first day of spring, total peace. This is what Adam saw. I am standing in the Garden of Eden.*

Jimmy took two steps toward the sound of the running water, hoping to find a nice shade tree to sit under. Before he got there, a voice like nothing he'd ever heard before boomed out behind him.

“NAME, PLEASE.”

Chapter Five

Jimmy turned to find himself staring into the Face of God—or at least how he had imagined God might look. A large man, chiseled face, long white beard that drooped to his waist, with eyes that saw all the way through Jimmy. He wore Ben Franklin-style glasses, and stood behind an ornate white podium perched on some form of elevation.

"Uhm, me?" Jimmy said.

"YES, SON, YOU." The voice was quiet, yet spoke with ultimate authority. Jimmy felt the words echo slightly inside his head.

Jimmy walked toward the podium. *That isn't a hill. God, if this is Him, looks to be ten feet tall. If this is supposed to intimidate me, it's working. I haven't felt like this since I put the tack on Mrs. Moss's chair in third grade, and got sent to Mr. Dinwiddie's office. He gave me a hack and told me that my behavior would go on my permanent record.*

Why do I get the sense that I'm about to deal with a much more permanent record than Mr. Dinwiddie's?

The giant stared impassively at Jimmy, waited a moment, then leaned forward and furrowed his brow. "I SAID: NAME, PLEASE." He was all business, and Jimmy was holding that business up.

Jimmy cleared his throat, hoping to find his voice. "Jimmy Velvet, sir. V-e-l-v-e-t."

The figure arched one tremendous eyebrow at Jimmy. *What made me think this God, or Whoever, needed my help with spelling?* The figure opened an impossibly huge book, so large it made an old-school Webster's dictionary look like a Harlequin romance paperback. He ran his finger down one page, tilting his head back a bit to look through the spectacles, then let forth a small, exasperated sigh. He was nearing the end of his infinite patience.

"IS THAT AN ALIAS, SON?" His voice had grown deeper, and more irritated.

Jimmy drew his breath in sharply. He had thought of himself as Jimmy Velvet for so long that for a moment he had trouble remembering his birth name. It finally snapped into his head.

"Sorry, sir. Yes. My name is James William Andrzejewski."

"AH. ANDRZEJEWSKI." *I shouldn't be surprised he pronounced it perfectly. Maybe God's Polish. If so, I hope that helps my cause.* "HERE YOU ARE. LET'S SEE NOW." Images flowed up from the book, dancing with lives of their own. *Reminds me of the hologram Princess Leia sent to Obi-Wan Kenobi in* Star Wars. Instead of a beautiful princess, though, the scenes came from Jimmy's life. A crystal-white aura surrounded each one.

That must be me as a baby, in my crib, Mom rocking me to sleep. There I am lying on the floor, fascinated with my toes. A lump materialized in his throat as Jimmy saw his young mother holding him close, eyes full of maternal adoration, saying: "Who's the best boy in the world? Yes, it's my Jimmy boy." He hadn't seen her in years, hadn't so much as talked to her on the phone. *And I never will again. I will never get to tell her goodbye.*

The very early days of Jimmy's life went by quickly. *Guess there wasn't much good or bad I could have done as a baby that mattered later on.* Many scenes were mundane: Jimmy walking to school, playing hide 'n seek with his friends, watching *Leave it to Beaver* and eating dinner with his parents off TV trays. Sometimes he saw himself laughing or crying, but mostly he just lived his life like any other kid who grew up in the '50s and '60s. The surrounding aura remained dazzling white.

So cool.. I haven't thought about most of this in years. Some of it I completely forgot. Soon enough, Jimmy was watching his teenage self, and things became more uncomfortable. He watched himself go into a drug store and shoplift a small stack of comic books, walking out of the store trying to look natural. He saw himself punch and taunt the weird little kid who lived down the street, for no particular reason.

Jimmy cringed when he saw himself walking in the woods behind his house with his BB gun. *Oh, crap. I know what's coming.* Early teen Jimmy walked toward a fat robin redbreast perched on a low branch. He raised the rifle to his shoulder and fired. He had always been a lousy shot, but not on that day. The robin fell to the ground like a stone.

Jimmy had felt so remorseful for killing the robin that he'd gone back and buried it where it fell, crying the whole time. The burial scene and his remorseful tears didn't make the cut, though, because new scenes started playing. He snuck a quick glance at the big man's face to check for reactions, but the mighty face remained impassive and focused on the events unfolding in front of him.

Not all the scenes were shameful. Jimmy watched himself working for hours, digging his mom a new flower bed as a Mother's Day surprise. He watched himself walk along some railroad tracks with a few friends. They yelled insults and taunts at the hobos camped near the tracks. Jimmy hadn't had the courage to make his friends stop, but later he raided his mom's cupboards and took the drifters some cans of chili and soup. The aura framing the scenes was still white, but not the brilliant white it had once been.

His later teen years' images bored Jimmy, at least until the part where he met Rollie and they formed the band. He smiled to see himself standing in front of a mirror, posing with the Harmony Stratotone guitar he'd gotten at the pawn shop. At first, he hadn't been able to afford to get the amp to go with it, so he spent hours in front of the mirror posturing and practicing his licks. When he finally scraped up the money to get the amp, the result was disappointing. No matter how good he looked playing it, he sounded awful. He had a good ear, though, and put in many hours of practice. In time, he made himself into quite a damned good guitarist.

There I am at my first few gigs. He would jump to the front of the stage, whip his arm around in a frenzy and hit notes that made dogs howl all over the neighborhood. *God, I loved that. At the time, I thought that if I could ever make money doing it, that would be heaven.*

He also watched himself pick up girl after girl at those early gigs, take each one for a ride in his old Chevy, and then drop them off at home with never a backward glance. *I always thought we were both getting what we wanted, so there was nothing wrong with the way I treated them. I'm not sure that's how the Big Guy will see it.*

The images showed Jimmy promising to call each woman soon, then showed them sitting by the phone waiting for him to keep his commitments. He saw lots of tears, a couple of thrown household objects, in one case a vinyl record broken over a shapely thigh, profanities rained upon the entire male gender, and eyes grown cynical. *Da...darn. They believed me. I touched a lot of girls' lives, and not in a good way.*

The aura darkened.

Once The Black Velvets started their endless tour of Pacific Northwest back roads, everything looked like a series of reruns. Only the faces changed. Jimmy watched the bus rides, cheap motels, gigs and groupies, then more of the same. This bored Jimmy, but didn't seem to bore the Big Man. Jimmy saw himself drink more and more as whatever non-band interests he'd had dwindled away.

Then Debbie came into the picture. Jimmy felt something jab in his heart at his first sight of her, dancing in front of the stage at the Aces and Deuces. She looked so fresh, young and beautiful. *And I'm not going to like the rest of this, but I have a feeling that looking away isn't going to score me any points.* He watched the whole self-destructive soap opera all the way through. From this perspective, all the answers seemed clear, and at the time he'd missed them all. When he watched Debbie give the ultimatum and had to watch himself not give a shit, Jimmy finally had to turn away. The callous fool in the images didn't reconcile with the self-image he'd built up to shut out reality.

The aura surrounding the pictures had degraded into a sickly dark brown streaked with black. All the initial snowy white was gone.

The images weren't confined to the events Jimmy attended. He watched Debbie in the hospital giving birth to Emily. She was surrounded by friends and family, but when her pain was the worst, she had cried Jimmy's name. That image cut back and forth with a picture of him playing a gig in Dayton, Washington, flirting with a blonde in a denim miniskirt.

Jimmy hung his head. *I get it. I'm a complete shit heel. No more evidence is needed.*

Just as Jimmy was ready to beg 'no more,' the show came full circle. He watched The Black Velvets play that final night before the pathetic crowd at The Eagle's Nest. He watched the boring bus ride, interrupted by moments of terror and frenzy as he and Rollie tried to keep the bus on the road.

He watched the bus take out the guardrail, make an almost graceful jump, and hit the river. It sent a huge sheet of water before it as it struck, like a dinosaur version of how kids would flip water at each other in the swimming pool. There was the chaos of the crash, his efforts to make sure everyone got out. *Wow. Something good. Everyone but me managed to get to the riverbank. Rollie won't be along behind me here, or J.J.*

The final picture depicted Jimmy, struggling to reach the surface and draw breath. At the very last moment, he saw a sense of peace and acceptance wash over his face. The surrounding frame had lightened considerably, then faded to nothingness. The old man closed the book. Jimmy expected to see hellfire and scorn in his eyes. Instead, he saw sympathy and understanding.

"SON, GOD GAVE YOU MANY GIFTS. HE GAVE YOU A GOOD MIND, AN ABLE BODY AND THE

ABILITY TO MAKE MUSIC. YOU NEGLECTED THOSE GIFTS AND WORKED TO DESTROY THE BODY HE GAVE YOU."

Jimmy had been dressed down by experts before, but nothing had impacted him like those few words. *You know, in life, I never knew remorse like this. So this is what I should have felt, and never did. It's caught up with me.* Jimmy hoped that the next thing he would say was something like 'YOU'RE GOING TO RECEIVE ONE MORE CHANCE TO GET IT RIGHT,' but in his heart he knew he'd used up all the chances. This was nothing more nor less than a final accounting for his life's deeds.

"YOU CHOSE TO LIVE YOUR LIFE IN A COWARDLY WAY, TAKING THE EASY WAY OUT OF EVERY SITUATION. YOU WERE SELF-INDULGENT AND THOUGHTLESS TOWARD OTHERS. I SEE GOODNESS IN YOUR HEART, BUT WHEN YOU HAD OPPORTUNITIES TO ACT ON THAT GOODNESS, YOU CHEATED YOURSELF OUT OF DOING SO." He paused, then continued: "AT THE SAME TIME, YOU DID WORK HARD TO DEVELOP THE GIFT OF MUSIC THAT GOD GAVE YOU. YOU ALSO GAVE UNSELFISHLY OF YOUR VERY LIFE TO SAVE ANOTHER. THAT DID MUCH TO BALANCE THE SCALES OF YOUR LIFE."

A moment of hope sprang up inside Jimmy.

"HOWEVER, EXCEPT IN EXTRAORDINARY CIRCUMSTANCES, NO ACTION AT THE END OF A LIFE CAN REVERSE A LIFETIME'S TRUE COURSE." He drew himself up to his full, incredible height, braced himself against his podium with both hands and said: "JAMES WILLIAM ANDREZEJEWSKI, I HAVE EXAMINED YOUR LIFE AND CONSIDERED IT CAREFULLY. I CANNOT FIND MERIT ENOUGH IN THAT LIFE TO PASS YOU INTO HIS PRESENCE AND THE KINGDOM OF HEAVEN."

True fear smothered Jimmy's small pang of hope. If Heaven was real, could Hell be far away?

"HOWEVER, YOU HAVE EXTENUATING CIRCUMSTANCES

THAT WILL SAVE YOU FROM THE CONSUMING ETERNAL FIRE. IN REVIEWING YOUR LIFE, I SEE YOU SPENT MUCH OF YOUR EARTHLY TIME PLAYING MUSIC. I ASSUME IT WAS ROCK 'N ROLL MUSIC?"

That feels like Aristotle chatting about NASCAR. It never occurred to me that God would give a damn about rock 'n roll. I could see Him throwing some damns right at it, and I guess I was the poster child. I think I'm sunk, twice in one day, but let's see what 'extenuating circumstances' means. Could be a loophole. "Yes. I played rock 'n roll, sir," said Jimmy, with as much dignity as he could muster.

The figure nodded. "THAT BEING THE CASE, YOU HAVE A CHOICE TO MAKE. I MIGHT ADD," he said, lowering his voice as if to confide, "THAT IS SOMETHING MANY PEOPLE WHO HAVE STOOD IN YOUR POSITION WOULD HAVE LIKED TO HAVE. HE WHO HAS NO NAME, IN INFINITE WISDOM, CREATED NEW UNIVERSES TO HOUSE WAYWARD SOULS WHO DID NOT EARN ENTRY INTO HEAVEN BUT DID NOT DESERVE SATAN'S ETERNAL COMPANY. ONE OF THOSE UNIVERSES IS SUITABLE FOR YOU. WE HAVE NO NAME FOR THESE UNIVERSES, BUT ANOTHER HUMAN HAS NAMED THIS ONE 'ROCK 'N ROLL HEAVEN.'"

Jimmy had been listening on the assumption his whole existence depended on it. *Is this a joke? Fool, do you really think this guy is going to go all wiseass at a time like this?*

"MAKE YOUR CHOICE NOW. GO EITHER TO YOUR EARNED ETERNITY OR THE ALTERNATIVE UNIVERSE."

Jimmy had faced many difficult questions in his lifetime. This was not one of them.

"I'll take Rock 'n Roll Heaven, sir."

The ghost of a smile played across the big man's lips, soon replaced by the same inscrutable, blank expression. He nodded and raised his hand like a desk clerk summoning a bellhop.

A handsome young man with long, curly brown hair appeared at his side. Literally, appeared. One minute, not there.

The next, there.

"Yes, sir?" asked the young man, tone and posture completely deferential.

After a brief up and down inspection, the old man said "PERTIME, THIS IS JIMMY VELVET. JIMMY IS THE NEWEST CITIZEN OF ROCK 'N ROLL HEAVEN. I KNOW YOU LIKE IT THERE, SO I WANT YOU TO ESCORT HIM. HELP HIM FEEL AT HOME."

"Yes, of course, sir," Pertime said. He was still carefully inspecting the patch of grass at his feet.

The old man knelt down, so that his head was at Jimmy's eye level. His eyes became kind. He locked eyes with Jimmy. *I feel safe here. Maybe he'd let me stay.* Jimmy started toward him, but didn't get a word out. The old man said, gently, "I HOPE YOU FIND EVERYTHING YOU ARE LOOKING FOR."

Then he was gone.

Chapter Six

Jimmy stood silent, stunned, trying to process. After a few seconds, he realized that Pertime was not only still with him, the guide was saying something.

"...so, yeah, he loves to do that disappearing bit with the new arrivals. They're the only ones he can still impress with it, I guess."

Though nowhere near the size of the Big Guy, as Jimmy had begun to think of him, Pertime was a head taller than Jimmy's six feet. He wore a plain white robe with a brown corded sash and was a little on the thin side, like a handsome, ascetic monk. His long curly hair fell loosely around his shoulders. He smiled companionably.

I have seen this face before. I know it. Where the f...yes. Michelangelo's David. "Are... are you an angel?"

"Oh, you mean like this?"

Rays of golden light surrounded Pertime. Large white wings sprouted out his back and he rose up until he was floating a foot off the ground. He held his hands folded in front of him, affecting a solemn, pious expression on his beautiful face.

"Yeah. That's what I mean," Jimmy said, knowing how stupid he sounded.

"I am what you have heard referred to as an angel, but I hardly ever look like this. This is more what I would call my Sunday best. I just use it for parades and impressing dignitaries and such."

Is this guy serious?

Pertime floated gently back to the ground and lost the wings, golden light and the pious expression. "Well, come on," he said.

“How far is it?” Jimmy asked, because it seemed like something to ask.

“There’s no answer to that. Time and space are meaningless here. That means nothing is very far away, but there’s no way to tell how long it’ll take to get there. See, here we are.”

Jimmy looked ahead and felt like Dorothy in *The Wizard of Oz*. Their path led into a narrow road made of yellow somethings, and this clearly was not Kansas.

Before long, the road widened and passed under a big arching billboard. On the billboard was a marquee; not an electronic one, but the old-fashioned kind where you changed the letters using a long pole with a suction cup on the end. *I wonder whose job it is to change the sign? Kind of hard to imagine an angel with a pole in his hands, spelling out the words.* The reader board said:

WELCOME TO ROCK 'N ROLL HEAVEN!

Yeah, we’ve got a hell of a band!

TONITE! JIMMY ‘GUITAR’ VELVET'S OPENING NIGHT WITH SPECIAL GUESTS TBA!

CAN MUSIC SAVE YOUR SOUL?

It was a slice of late 1950s Americana. The golden street led gently down to what looked like a little town where Hollywood could have filmed *The Ozzie and Harriet Show* or *Leave it To Beaver*.

“So, is this really Rock ‘n Roll Heaven?”

“The sign would seem to suggest that, wouldn't you agree?” Pertime chuckled.

“Are all the dead rock stars from earth are here?”

“Not all of them, but for the most part, yes.”

“Elvis.”

“Yes.”

"John Lennon?”

"Mm-hmm."

"Buddy Holly?"

"Oh, yes. He was The First."

"Jim Morrison?"

"Yes."

"Okay, then. Here's what I don't understand. If all those guys are in this place, not to mention Jimi Hendrix, or Ritchie Valens, or Roy Orbison, or Randy Rhoads...why am I a headliner? Every one of those guys is a legend, people that could pack any house, anytime, anywhere. I'm not even a has-been. I'm a never-was. There's no way I can headline in a place like this. I don't qualify to play my guitar for change on the sidewalk in front of any of those shows, much less open for them. I might qualify to help haul their equipment, if they were feeling real generous."

Pertime smiled beatifically. "Two things: one, everyone's Opening Night is headlined on the billboard, no matter who they are and how big they were or weren't on earth. It's a way of welcoming everyone here. Two, in Rock 'n Roll Heaven, there are different standards in effect. You've been judged. That is behind you. In Rock 'n Roll Heaven, what people think about you will be based on how you play and how much you put into your music. We have been watching you for a long time. We believe you're going to do very well here. Speaking of here, this is the beginning of the road to Rock 'n Roll Heaven."

"Why in the world were you watching me?"

Pertime smiled again. "I know this looks like what you would call Heaven, but the souls who live here aren't always happy with the way things are. There's a legend here that says that a 'never-was,' as you call yourself, would make things right here. A lot of people are interested in meeting you."

"If they're excited to meet me, I'm afraid they're going to be disappointed. When I was still on Earth, my dad always told me I didn't know my ass from a hole in the ground. I couldn't even manage to fix myself, so I don't see how I'll be fixing anyone or anything else."

Pertime shrugged and gestured down at the golden road that led toward town. Now that they were at its edge, Jimmy could see the road wasn’t actually made of yellow bricks, but of gold records. Not the plain old gold kind one saw hanging in a recording studio, but luminescent golden records that glowed like fireflies on a warm summer evening. Their accumulated light cast an odd, slightly eerie glow over the entrance to Rock ‘n Roll Heaven.

Jimmy kneeled down at the edge of the road and read the labels nearest him. The first record he saw was *Rock Around the Clock* by Bill Haley and His Comets. Right next to that was *Be-Bop-A-Lula* by Gene Vincent and His Blue Caps. Next to that was *No Particular Place to Go* by Chuck Berry.

Jimmy reached out and touched that one. As soon as he did, the music swelled up in his head, originating within it. He heard Chuck Berry singing and playing in perfect stereo. He pulled his hand away in surprise; the music in his head stopped instantly.

“Well, that’s all kinds of cool, but if I hear every one of those songs when I step on them, this trick’s going to get old fast.” Pertime didn’t say anything, but watched Jimmy step onto the golden road. *No music. Thank God. So to speak.*

Pertime laid a hand on Jimmy’s shoulder and pointed him toward town. They walked side by side down the golden road, with Jimmy occasionally kneeling down to hear a great song like *Come Go With Me* by the Del Vikings, or *Bring It on Home to Me* by Sam Cooke.

Music seemed to be everywhere. A slight breeze rustled through tall elms lining the road, sounding like a whisper of “Sh-Boom, Sh-Boom." Crickets, frogs and birds combined for a soft chorus that reminded Jimmy of the melody of *Smoke Gets in Your Eyes.*

Jimmy and Pertime walked under the billboard, past the trees and turned a corner into a sleepy little town. It was nothing fancy. It looked like a fully realized set for the play *Our Town*.

None of the buildings were more than two stories tall. They

all seemed to be made out of brick or stucco. All the windows looked freshly washed; the sidewalk was clean. They walked past a drug store, a five and dime, a small bookstore and a movie theater whose marquee read THE BLACKBOARD JUNGLE. There were people here and there on the sidewalk, but Jimmy and Pertime had the Golden Road to themselves. There were no cars or bikes. The air smelled of new-mown lawn, and Jimmy could feel warmth on his face, despite the absence of a sun.

Jimmy craned his neck, looking at everyone, hoping to recognize somebody; maybe Eddie Cochran, or Bobby Fuller, or Elvis disguised as a short-order cook. He didn't recognize a single face. No one was paying them any attention.

Pertime seemed to read his mind. "Not exactly what you thought, huh, Jimmy? Just give it a chance. Every single person has a reason to be here, including a lot of non-musicians. There are engineers, record producers, roadies, even accountants. They might not be famous, but there's logic to it. You'll see. There's the first stop on our tour, just up ahead."

Ahead on the right was an impossibly huge skating rink. Except for the sheer size, it fit right in with the rest of the town. It had a plain wooden exterior that looked freshly painted, tan with white trim. There were four sets of glass double doors at the front of the building. Overhead, a hand-painted sign read: *"Appearing Nightly – The Lubbock Flash – Buddy Holly, with Special Guests Ritchie Valens and J.P. Richardson."*

A shiver ran down Jimmy's spine.

He walked up to one of the doors and cupped his hands around his eyes so he could see inside. It was what it looked like: a massive skating rink. In the middle of the skating oval was an elevated wooden stage with hay bales scattered carelessly around. Most of the stage was empty, except for a Gibson acoustic guitar with lettering across the bottom that read *Texas*, an electric Fender Stratocaster leaning against an amp, a standup bass and a small drum kit.

Nobody's played rock 'n roll with a set-up like that for

twenty-five years. The whole thing looks like it should be in a museum, or the Rock 'n Roll Hall of Fame. It was all so casually laid out that it looked like the players might reappear at any moment and start a set.

Without thinking, Jimmy reached down to open the door and go in for a closer look. It was locked. *Damn.* Jimmy never would have handled anyone else's guitar without permission, but he would have loved to get a better look at them.

Jimmy was lost in his thoughts, imagining being inside when the music was playing, watching Buddy Holly blast out *That'll Be the Day*, when a hand on his shoulder pulled him out of his reverie.

Jimmy turned around and looked directly into the trademark black-framed glasses and dark brown eyes of Charles Hardin "Buddy" Holly. He was wearing a plain white t-shirt and jeans pegged at the ankles, curly dark hair spilling over his forehead. Buddy had died February 3rd, 1959, Jimmy's tenth birthday, so Jimmy had missed out on seeing him in person. He was taller and thinner than Jimmy would have guessed.

Jimmy jerked to a stop, disoriented, trying to make sense of it. Standing less than three feet away was the legend himself, still looking exactly like the twenty-two-year-old he had been on the day the music died. Every other miracle he had seen up to that point faded into insignificance. *It is all I can do not to scream, "Holy shit! Do you know who you are?"*

"Say, Jimmy. I didn't mean to scare you. You all right?" Buddy's speaking voice was deeper than Jimmy would have thought, but the Texas drawl was there in force.

"Uhhh…"

Pertime took mercy on Jimmy and jumped in to fill the void. "Jimmy, this is Buddy Holly. Buddy, please meet Jimmy 'Guitar' Velvet."

Buddy smiled so kindly at Jimmy it put him halfway at ease. "Howdy, Jimmy. Pleased to meet you."

The very first song the Velvets had played at their first gig was Buddy's *Heartbeat.* The last set he'd ever played, at The

Eagle's Nest, had included his own version of *That'll be the Day. Tell me I'm now dead, that I can handle. Tell me I'm standing in front of Buddy freaking Holly? Someone has to be out of their mind. Might be me. Well, I guess there's one thing worse than making an ass of myself, and that's making an ass of myself in front of my idol.* Jimmy cleared his throat. "Umm, pleased to meet you Buddy. I…I don't know what to say."

"You don't need to say anything." Buddy said. "I just dropped by to see if maybe you wanted to come in and see my place, maybe play together a little bit."

That confirms it. I now believe I am definitely in Heaven. "Of course I would!" Jimmy blurted, half star struck and a little too loudly.

Buddy laughed and said, "Well, c'mon then, let's go on in." Buddy reached his hand out and pushed the door that had been locked a moment before. It whooshed open.

Pertime laid a hand on Jimmy's shoulder and dropped his voice. "Don't worry. Most everybody's a little dazzled when they first meet Buddy. Even John Lennon got a little twisted up when he met him, and almost nothing impresses John."

Buddy walked inside and to the left, flipping a row of switches. The whole interior lit up. A faint buzz emanated from the overhead fluorescent lights.

"It ain't fancy, but I like it." Buddy said.

"So do I." The air smelled of popcorn and floor oil, like the roller rink near Grandma's house. Wheel marks decorated the circular floor. Nothing was easier than picturing hundreds of skating couples holding hands, skating in rhythm to Buddy Holly playing live.

"Everybody that headlines in Rock 'n Roll Heaven gets their own place. We'll talk about yours coming up. This is Buddy's," Pertime said.

"Everyone gets to choose their own layout, and I liked this. I knew I was going to spend a lot of time here, so I wanted it to be comfortable. I never did go in too much for all that neon and fancy lighting and stuff. I leave that up to some of the other guys. We play here, most every night, pretty much like me and the boys used to in Lubbock before we made it big."

"Usually, J.P.—the Big Bopper—comes out and does a quick warm-up set, then Ritchie does his set. After that, I do a set with this little trio I've put together, and then we all come out and jam until everybody's ready to go home. J.P. and Ritchie could have had their own places, but when we got here, the whole place was empty, so we just decided to stick together right here."

God. Just try and be cool, will you? "Can I just hang out here, then? I'd give anything to see that show."

"Jimmy, you can come and play with us any time you want, but we won't be playing tonight. There's only one ticket in town, and that's you, hoss. Every other show in town will be dark tonight except yours. I did want to ask you something, though."

"What's that?"

"Would you mind if I came and sat in with you?"

I. Have. No. Words.

Then find some! "You want to come and sit in with me? I...Buddy, you're my hero. You're the reason I wanted to pick up a guitar. All the other kids wanted to be Elvis, but I wanted to be you. The day your plane went down..." *Oh, shit. Maybe it's bad manners to mention someone's real-life death. Hope not, or that he'll forgive me.* "...anyway, that was my birthday, and my mom let me stay home from school because I was so upset. I remember..." Jimmy realized he was babbling, and decided to shut up.

Buddy smiled at him. "I'll take that for a 'yes' then, huh? Well, that'll be great. We'll get you off to a good start. Pertime and I'll take you around to meet a few of the other guys, and you can figure out who you want for the rest of your band."

As Jimmy's head was filling with the possibilities, Buddy hopped nimbly onto the stage. "Let's get a head start on the whole thing right now, whaddya say?"

Buddy slipped the strap of his Stratocaster over his head.

"Let's see, there's got to be another guitar around here somewhere." He slid his Strat over his back and rummaged around in a storage area at the side of the stage. After much rattling, some humming, and a small crash, he emerged with another guitar just like the one he was holding.

"Reckon this'll do for now," Buddy drawled. Jimmy climbed up on the stage and strapped on the offered guitar. It fit as if he had already adjusted it.

Buddy strummed a few random chords, then looked thoughtful."Hey, let's see if you know this one." He jumped right into the *a cappella*, hiccupping vocal that led off *Rave On.* He played the lead guitar part, sang, and gestured for Jimmy to join in.

Jimmy stood stock still, wearing Buddy Holly's spare guitar, watching the legend. He had sung *Rave On* hundreds of times in his career, but at that moment, he couldn't remember the chord progression. Buddy kept waving for Jimmy to jump in with him, and on the second chorus, he tried. All that came out was an embarrassing little croak. *I'm humiliating myself!* Jimmy just strummed along, trying to catch his breath.

Pertime stood off to the side, leaning against an amp, watching Jimmy and tapping his foot slightly. Buddy strode around the stage, smiling.

That's exactly how rock 'n roll is supposed to make you feel.

Jimmy's paralysis melted away. The chords popped back into his head like they had been there all along, and he played what he decided was passable backup. Where the song could have ended, Buddy brought it back around again, but nodded his head to throw the lead vocals to Jimmy.

When Jimmy had done this song in the clubs, he had done it Buddy-style. Halfway through, he was bending his syllables just right, and they even managed some nice two-part harmonies on the chorus. It was over too soon for Jimmy's taste, but they managed to both stop playing at the same time, which is a desirable ending for a rock 'n roll song.

I think that's the worst I've played since that first kegger. And nothing I played ever felt so good.

Jimmy wiped his forehead and leaned against one of the hay bale stacks. Buddy was having none of that. “C’mon, old man, you can’t be that out of shape, can you? One song and you’re done? Let’s do another one. Here we go, you should know this one…”

Buddy laid down the classic lick that jump-starts *Johnny B. Goode.* The next thing he knew, Jimmy was back in the middle of the stage, trading guitar parts and jumping around like a kid.

Buddy led Jimmy through *Brown Eyed Handsome Man, Summertime Blues, That’s Alright, Mama* and *Party Doll.* By the end of the set, it felt like jamming with any other rock ‘n roller. Any other rock ‘n roller that played and sang like Buddy Holly, anyway.

“Are you two finished for now?” Pertime asked. “Rock ‘n roll was never meant to be played this early in the day. Let’s go.”

“Okay, Per,” said Buddy, toweling the sweat off his face. “Let me get my guitars ready to be shipped to Jimmy’s place and we’ll be ready.” Buddy gave Jimmy a quick wink and pulled two guitar cases out of the storage area. One was a sturdy black case with hinges in the back. He took his Strat, unplugged it from the amp and placed it gently in the case. The second case was hand-tooled brown leather, and he laid the Gibson acoustic inside. *He handles them like women...like I should have handled women in life. I know that way. That's love. Those aren't just wood and string to him.*

While Buddy packed, Jimmy absently strummed the guitar in his hands. He didn’t want to take it off. This didn’t seem like the right time to ask Buddy if he could borrow it until he found one of his own, though, so he slipped it off and leaned it carefully against the amp. Every piece of equipment on the stage fit right into Buddy's lifetime. There were no wireless pick-ups, no neckless basses. *Is that a rule here, or is that just how Buddy and his fellow legends like it?*

Buddy had finished readying his guitars. He looked at Jimmy. “Ready?”

“Come on, Jimmy,” Pertime said. “We’ve got all of Rock ‘n Roll Heaven still ahead of us today. Don’t you want to see what other wonders await us?”

He did.

Chapter Seven

Jimmy and Pertime stood outside in what felt like a perfect spring morning, waiting for Buddy to finish up inside the rink and join them. Jimmy was still gazing inside, processing it all.

"Since Buddy arrived on the very first day Rock 'n Roll Heaven was created, he's felt a responsibility to make sure he's the first person everybody meets," Pertime said. "He likes to help them shake the cobwebs out and jam a little if they want. Most everybody seems to get a kick out of it."

"*Most* everybody? I can't imagine there's anybody that's not blown away to meet Buddy Holly, let alone get a chance to play with him."

"The requirements for getting in to Rock 'n Roll Heaven are looser than for the main Heaven itself. The only requirement is that you played or were involved with rock 'n roll music while you were on earth. Some of the people you're going to meet had the option of going to regular heaven, but chose this." Pertime lowered his voice, "Buddy did."

Jimmy remembered the intensity of the old man's gaze and the feeling the light had stirred inside him. *I don't know if I could have ever walked away from that, no matter what was waiting here.*

"That means," Pertime continued, "there are a lot of great people that wouldn't be here otherwise. At the same time, there's nothing to keep the jerks out, either."

Buddy strolled out the door. He had changed into a sharp grey suit and sunglasses, just as if he'd stepped off the cover of one of his albums. The trio set off down the golden street, with Pertime and Buddy chatting quietly in the lead. Jimmy played the gawking tourist. He continually peeked down at the records he was walking on. *At some point, those have to repeat. There are only so many song titles, right?* But, like snowflakes, none did.

Their path moved away from the small-town business district housing Buddy's roller rink, toward a section of larger buildings. As they walked under an awning, Jimmy glanced through a large picture window and saw a man sitting at a 1950s radio board with half a dozen potentiometers, two turntables and a hanging microphone. Above the sidewalk, speakers broadcast what he was playing. The last few notes of The Fleetwoods' *Come Softly* faded out.

"This is Alan Freed, King of the Moondoggers, playing the songs that matter, the records that have stood the test of time and crossed over with me to Rock 'n Roll Heaven. These are the Moonglows, from Cleveland, Ohio, waaaay back in the ole US of A." He pushed a button and the record started to spin. The doo-wop intro of *Sincerely* played, with just a hint of scratchiness as the 45 turned.

"That's Alan Freed!"

"Yeah, it is," Buddy drawled. "You can't be surprised to see Alan in Rock 'n Roll Heaven. He doesn't have a regularly scheduled show, but he goes on the air whenever he wants."

Alan looked out the window and waved as he cued up the next record. By the time they were out of earshot, *Sincerely* had finished playing and segued directly into *Mr. Lee* by The Bobbettes.

Ahead, Jimmy saw his first neon sign of Rock 'n Roll Heaven: a brightly lit cartoon version of a shark, wearing a tuxedo and top hat. The shark was smiling, baring his long row of sparkling white teeth. Over the shark, blinking red letters spelled out 'Mac's.' Jimmy looked at Pertime. "Whose place is this?"

"Come on, Jimmy," said the angel in a *get real, man* tone. "We're in the '50s section of Rock 'n Roll Heaven and here's a big nightclub called 'Mac's.' Whose club could that be?"

The light dawned. "Of course. Bobby Darin. *Mac the*

Knife.” Duh. Be kind to the slow-witted, Pertime.

“But I remember seeing a Bobby Darin television special in the '70s. I don’t remember when he died, but it sure wasn’t the ‘50s. How come his place is here?”

“When you think of Bobby Darin, what songs do you think about?”

Jimmy had never included any of Darin’s songs in his sets. He had to think. “Let’s see, I remember *Splish Splash, Dream Lover*, and *Beyond the Sea*, along with *Mac the Knife.”*

“Right," said Pertime, as though teaching a child. "And when did all those songs come out?”

“The late fifties, I guess.”

“Exactly. That’s why Bobby wanted his place here. He could’ve put it up ahead, with the guys from the sixties, or even the seventies. He felt like he belonged here, so this is where he stays. Here’s another way to look at it. Fats Domino is still alive, right?”

“Yes, I saw him at Bumbershoot in Seattle not too long ago, and he seemed pretty lively to me.”

“Okay. When his time eventually comes, if he decides to come here, where do you think he’ll want to be? Alongside Iron Maiden and the other '70s metal bands he's outliving? The new wave artists from the '80s? Unlikely. I expect he’ll want to be right here, with his friends and people who know how to make the same kind of music he did. Everybody gets to decide where they belong, and where they want to put their own club.”

“Where should mine be, then? I’m not sure I even have an era I can call my own. I played everything from the '50s right up to songs that were written the same year I died. I played anything that I thought would bring us a paycheck big enough to get us to the next gig.”

Buddy spoke up. “That’s one of the reasons we’re taking this tour—so you can figure out where you belong. C’mon, let’s see if we can find Bobby.”

Mac’s looked huge on the outside, but when they stepped through the glass double doors, it felt more like an intimate, smoky night club. It was the kind of place that the British Invasion of the '60s swept out of fashion. It was dark inside, but it felt good to Jimmy. *Like a ritzy Vegas showroom from the Rat Pack days.* There was no bar in sight. The whole room was filled with half-oval high-back booths, upholstered in soft leather and accented with crushed velvet and polished chrome trim. The booths were arranged on different levels throughout the club, all facing a large burgundy curtain. The aisles between the booths were covered in deep pile carpeting, defined by a row of softly glowing lights embedded in the floor.

The club was deserted except for one lone figure sauntering up the main aisle. He wore a perfectly tailored tuxedo with the collar open at the neck. When the light struck the handsome face and the casually brushed-back black hair, Jimmy saw laughing eyes of the sort that accompanied a joke waiting on the telling. Jimmy had never been as big a fan of Bobby Darin as he had been of Buddy, or Roy Orbison or Jim Morrison, but he still thrilled to see the man walking straight toward him.

"Hey, fellas, what's up? I didn't know you'd be around today, Per. How's it going, Buddy?"

Bobby Darin had been born in Harlem and raised in the Bronx, but all traces of that accent had long evaporated. His voice was smooth and melodious. Both Buddy and Pertime reached out and shook his hand.

"Bobby," Pertime said, "this is Jimmy Velvet. He's a new arrival, so I'm taking him on the tour. I thought he'd enjoy meeting you and seeing your place."

"Well, all right, Jimmy. I'm pleased to meet you. I'm sorry to say I'm not familiar with your music. You must have come along after I was gone."

That makes sense. I should expect that from everyone. He's trying not to be rude. "Actually, I'd already had my band together for a few years when you uhhh..." *Speaking of not being rude. How do I refer to a man's death, to his face?*

"It's all right, Jimmy, don't worry about it," he said with

his trademark lopsided grin. "Other than guys like this," gesturing at Pertime, "the one thing we've all got in common is that we all died. No point being embarrassed about the price of admission."

I am anyway. And it's not like I can lie here. That ability died. "Well, then...I'd already had my band together for a few years before you died. I never broke out of the bar scene. I was still playing in dives right up to the very end."

Bobby perked up. "Is that right? Well, that doesn't matter here, Jimmy. Come on in the back and I'll introduce you to some of the other fellas that're hanging around. During the day, when everything is dark, there's real work that can be done if you're the type, but we just hang around and drink coffee and play cards. We started playing music because we didn't want to do real work!"

Bobby led the way around the side of the stage to a black door that swung open into a labyrinth of hallways and rooms. They soon emerged into a cozy, well-lit room.

"I remember my first day here," Bobby continued, "I wasn't lucky to get Pertime like you are. I got this stuffy old angel named Margent who was so uptight, if you stuck a piece of coal up his butt, you'd have a diamond in no time."

Bobby winked at Buddy. Pertime studied the ceiling. If he pretended not to hear, he wouldn't have to pretend to be offended.

"He introduced me to Buddy first thing, all right, but he said something like 'You may know something of this young man. He is said to have an excellent reputation in the type of music that is going to be played here.' Hell, Margent wouldn't have known rock 'n roll if it had risen up and bit him on his holy butt."

"I figured he must have ticked somebody off and got sent here as punishment, because he didn't like it one bit," Buddy said, smiling at the memory.

Pertime was now examining his perfectly manicured fingernails, losing the battle against a small smile.

The room had functional grey carpet and unfinished walls, giving a backstage impression. Against one wall rested a large overstuffed sofa, across from a couple of easy chairs. In the middle of the room was a table with six straight-backed chairs, four occupied.

The occupants were young men in their early twenties, casually dressed, each holding a handful of cards. There was an unclaimed hand in front of the fifth chair, which Jimmy assumed Bobby had just abandoned. Bobby Darin looked like he had just stepped offstage and loosened his tie, but the other four were dressed much more casually—T-shirts or short sleeve casual shirts and blue jeans. *Those are not just kids, hanging around, killing time.. This is Rock 'n Roll Heaven. My god, I recognize three of them.*

"Hey, guys, this is Jimmy Velvet," Bobby said. "Pertime and Buddy are taking him on the nickel tour. Jimmy, you might remember some of these old-timers. Eddie Cochran, Gene Vincent, Ritchie Valens and Danny Rapp."

Who the h...yeah. Danny and the Juniors. I used to have an old 45 of At the Hop *when I was about ten, with a picture sleeve. Dead ringer.*

They look so young.

Eddie Cochran had only been twenty-two when he died. Ritchie Valens had been seventeen. Gene Vincent had been older, though, and Danny Rapp had lived into his forties. Here, they all looked young enough to have been in high school or college.

"Hi, guys," Jimmy said. "It feels strange to say it, since I'm about twice your age, but I grew up listening to you. The first rock 'n roll song I ever heard live was *Summertime Blues*. It's a real pleasure to meet you all."

Eddie Cochran stood up from the table, said "Great, maybe we can jam on it sometime. I've heard some pretty wild versions of my old song since I got here." He shook Jimmy's hand with both of his.

"You made music that felt good." Jimmy said in a heartfelt

tone.

“It’s nice of you to say that, Jimmy. We feel the same way about our music. After our time, a lot of the honesty went out of it. Since you grew up listening and playing our music, we’d love to have you settle down here with us. There’s a bunch of great guys here and I think you’d like it. Whadya say, guys?”

Everyone around the table indicated assent, and they all got up to come shake hands with Jimmy. “Hold on, now, boys,” Pertime said. “Jimmy’s just getting started here. Give him a little room to breathe before he makes that decision.” *What a feeling. They accept me, the nobody, as one of their own. Maybe here, I'm not going to be such a nobody.*

Jimmy shook each man's hand. “Thanks, fellas. I can’t wait.”

“All right,” Pertime said. “We’ve got a schedule to keep.”

"You need a watch you can keep looking at, Pertime," said Buddy Holly. There were smiles and snickers.

Pertime led the way back through the maze of turns until they were back in the dark interior of the showroom. Jimmy paused in front of the stage, where one brilliant, white spotlight lit the curtain. *I can’t imagine what it’s like to be in this audience? These guys laid down the roots of all that I love and am. Not was, either. Am.*

When they walked out into the warm, fragrant air, Jimmy got that slight feeling of displacement he could remember from emerging out of Saturday movie matinées into full daylight. His internal clock was saying it should be getting dark, but the ambient light hadn't changed. Something was off.

“Hey, Pertime. All those guys in there looked like they were about the same age, but that can’t be right. Ritchie and Eddie were just kids when they died, but Gene Vincent was older, and I saw Danny Rapp at one of those rock ‘n roll revival shows in the early '80s. He had to be in his forties. What gives?”

“Like a lot of things in Rock ‘n Roll Heaven, Jimmy, there are rules. They are just different than what you were used to on Earth. On Earth, time is linear; you age in a direct line. Here, things are more flexible. You can choose to assume the physical body you had at any point during that span. The longer you lived on earth, the more choices you have. For example, Danny Rapp was in his forties when he died, but he knew he'd be hanging out with a bunch of friends like Eddie and Gene. He didn't want to feel like he was old enough to be their father, so he chose to be about the same age."

Jimmy let out a long, low, whistle. "You're saying I don't have to be stuck with this body anymore? I can get rid of my gray hair and aching back? If word of this ever got out, you guys would be swamped here. I know a lot of rockers that would gladly pay a little price like dying to get their lost youth back."

"Most people think that's one of the coolest things, all right," Buddy chimed in. "But there are still rules. Once you choose what age you want to be, you're pretty well stuck with it. There are exceptions, but it's really tough to get it changed."

"Yes," Pertime said. "You have to get an angel to sponsor the change, then they have to take it to the proper sub-committee to show valid reasons why the change should be made. If they agree, they take it to the full committee of archangels..."

"It's a pain in the butt, is what it is," Buddy interrupted. "It's better to pick an age you're going to be happy with for a long time, then stick with that."

Even Heaven has bureaucratic bullshit. Still, no point arguing about it. So what'll I do? Go back to my teens, but knowing what I know now, or maybe more like I was when he was twenty-five?

"When do I have to, or get to, make this momentous decision?"

"Not yet," Pertime said. "You've got a lot to consider first. Eternity's a long time." Buddy and Pertime exchanged an undecipherable glance, and they moved on.

The three walked by a '50s-style dance hall with a sign out front saying *Be-Bop. That'd be Gene Vincent, I'll bet.* Jimmy looked in as they passed. Almost the whole interior was made up of a huge dance floor with a small, simple stage at one end.

Next up was *The Four Aces*, and Jimmy couldn't figure out who it might belong to. "Alright, guys, I give up. Whose place is that?"

"*The Four Aces* is Bill Haley's place."

"Oh. I figured he would have a place called *Rock Around the Clock*, or *See You Later, Alligator*. Why'd he name it *Four Aces*?"

"Bill was a little older than most of the stars of the '50s. He was thirty when he put out *Rock Around the Clock*, and he'd had a pretty good career already. His first band was a western swing band that ended up being known as The Four Aces. He's always loved playing western swing, so he named his club for the old band. He mixes in a lot of different music when he plays. Never has any trouble packing the place."

Up next was an intimate nightclub called *Sax Appeal*. Jimmy shook his head, looked at his guides and shrugged his shoulders, stumped again.

"King Curtis...Curtis Ousley," Pertime said. "One of the greatest sax players ever. He's got his own place, but it's hardly ever open, because everyone's always talking him into sitting in. Curtis isn't very good at saying 'no.'"

As soon as Pertime mentioned King Curtis's name, Jimmy started nodding. *Maybe he'll come play with me. I feel like a greedy kid on Christmas morning, who already got a new BB gun, skateboard, guitar, bike, and now hopes there's also a telescope under the tree.*

Just ahead on the golden road was a wooden sign painted with "You're leaving the rockin' '50s. Are you sure you want to go?" Right after the sign, the road took a sharp turn. When they walked around it, Jimmy sucked in his breath. Ahead was the most immense castle he had ever seen.

"Holy shit!" Jimmy said before he could catch himself. "Who lives there?"

Chapter Eight

Pertime curled his lip back, deepened his voice and said "That's where the King lives, baby."

Even angels can't resist doing an Elvis imitation.

The castle was so tall that Jimmy had to crane his neck to look for the upper spires, which disappeared into the fluffy clouds above. The exterior was a dazzling white with polished gold accents. This was either the most perfect job of masonry ever, or the whole place had been molded rather than built. Crimson banners flew in a dozen different locations around the castle, emblazoned with a golden E.

"So what's the deal, are we going in?" Jimmy said.

Pertime cocked his head a little. "Not a big fan of the King, Jimmy?

Jimmy blushed a little. "Well, I guess I'm not the biggest fan. When he was changing rock 'n roll, I was too young to pay too much attention to him. By the time I was old enough to notice, he'd gotten shipped off to the army. When he came back, he made a bunch of crappy movies and sang songs like *Bossa Nova Baby.* He may have been 'The King' to my Mom, or my aunt Viv, but to me he was just another singer. Still, he was the biggest pop culture icon of the twentieth century, so I wouldn't skip the chance to meet him."

"I usually don't take people into the castle on their tours," Pertime said, "but I'll see what I can do."

Pertime walked over to an intercom next to the gigantic moat, pushed a button. "This is Pertime. We'd like to come in. Can you lower the drawbridge, please?"

There was a pause, then a few seconds of static before a not-quite-stifled giggle. A voice said "Pertime, who?"

So knock-knock jokes aren't too juvenile for Rock 'n Roll Heaven. Pertime rolled his eyes. "22? Is that you? Don't make me summon the lightning and smite you again. Let the drawbridge down, please."

'22'—whoever he was—must have taken Pertime seriously, because a drawbridge the size of a football field lowered ponderously toward them. "Careful to stand outside the marked area," Pertime cautioned. As they waited for the drawbridge to settle into place, Jimmy glanced around. It was cloudier here, and cooler too. The smell of fresh-mown lawn was gone, replaced by an antiseptic industrial cleaner smell. *And I miss the '50s already.*

"Pertime, who is '22?'"

"Oh, yes, I suppose I should explain that. That was Elvis 22 on the other end. He's a little bit of a jokester."

"I don't get it. Who's Elvis 22?"

"Have you ever been to Vegas?"

Jimmy nodded. "One long weekend. I didn't even need a room. I stayed up 72 hours straight. Vegas was a dangerous place for someone like me."

"You probably noticed there was an Elvis on just about every street corner, right?"

"Well, sure, there are Elvis impersonators everywhere, but wouldn't the real one be right here? Don't tell me he really is still alive and pumping gas with Jim Morrison in Sheboygan?"

"No, Elvis died all right, and he lives right here in Rock 'n Roll Heaven. He had a lot of impersonators over the years, some of whom were very dedicated. A number of them have died too. They started showing up here and we didn't know what to do with all of them. If we'd given them all places of their own, we would have had to start an Elvisville just to handle them all. So, we talked to Elvis, and he agreed to let them all come and stay with him. It's not like he's short on room or anything, and he's a generous guy."

The drawbridge locked into place with a satisfying *clunk.*

"Most Elvis impersonators specialized in a specific stage of his career when they were alive, so they do the same here. But here, they are allowed to make changes to their appearances, so they resemble him more. We got so many of them, and they all started to look alike, that we started giving them numbers. We're up to Elvis 59 here in Rock 'n Roll Heaven, and we expect more to come. Elvis keeps them all busy, though. They're his new Memphis Mafia."

"Some of them are so good," Buddy chimed in, "that Elvis sends them out to perform at his shows. Nobody catches on."

They walked into the castle, and Jimmy wished he had a pair of sunglasses. There was pure white carpeting on the floors; the walls and ceiling were the same gleaming white as the exterior. The foyer was big enough to land an airplane, and Jimmy realized he was gawking like an Iowa tourist set loose in Manhattan. "A black velvet Elvis painting would go perfectly in here," he said.

He heard a snicker off to his right. A voice said, "Good one, man, never heard that one before."

Jimmy turned to see Elvis Presley, looking exactly like he had when he got out of the Army. His jet black hair was combed back, but one perfect curl hung down over his forehead. He leaned jauntily against some kind of reception desk. "Ah'll have to pass that one on to E. Maybe he'll put one in."

Pertime turned and said "Hey, 22. How's life in the castle?"

"Livin' like a King, nothin' better. Speaking of which, are you guys looking for The Boss?"

"Yeah, we are," Buddy said. "We didn't plan on stopping originally, but Jimmy here is a real big fan and wanted to meet him."

Well, that answers that. You can lie in Rock 'n Roll Heaven and not get struck by lighting.

"Sure, sure," 22 said. "Come on, let's go see if we can find 'im."

Pertime turned to Jimmy. "Elvis has a rule about not allowing strangers past the front desk, so wait here and look around. We'll be right back."

Jimmy found himself on his own in Rock 'n Roll Heaven for the first time. The huge foyer felt like the registration area in one of those gigantic Vegas casinos. There were a lot of gaudy, expensive-looking vases, furniture and artwork, mostly overdone. *A little too garish for me, thanks.*

Listen to you, Jimmy Velvet. A decor snob in Castle Presley.

There was an immense archway to the left. Jimmy walked through it and gaped again. A golden throne sat atop a dais in front of a waterfall that flowed under the throne, then disappeared into a catch basin.

"I guess every king needs a throne," Jimmy said, shaking his head.

As soon as Jimmy approached, the room filled with a soft version of Elvis singing *Crying in the Chapel.* Maybe all they played in here was his gospel music. *Should I stick around to see if they'll play* You're the Devil in Disguise*? Nah. This is too much for me.* He retreated to the foyer to wait for Buddy and Pertime.

Now and then, he saw an Elvis moving around on one errand or another. Many were young Elvises, but he saw one that looked like the leather-clad Elvis of the '68 Comeback Special. There were even two fat Elvises strolling along together, lost in conversation. Jimmy thought he heard one of them mention a fried banana sandwich as they wandered away.

Jimmy was so lost in Elvis-watching that it took him a moment to notice that the youngest Elvis yet had snuck up on him. The eyes were impossibly penetrating for a seventeen-year-old kid.

"Man, you scared me a little," said Jimmy, peering closer. "And you're either the best Elvis impersonator I've ever seen, or you're the real deal."

The young Elvis shook his head and grinned that famous Elvis grin. "Nah. Everybody around here looks a lot like The Boss. Ah'm number 17, pleased to meet you. We don't get many strangers here in the castle. Can Ah help you find somebody?"

"I don't think so," Jimmy said. "I'm here with Pertime the angel and Buddy Holly, but they went off to find the real Elvis."

"Sure, Ah get it. Another stop on the tour. You an Elvis fan?"

"It seems a little weird to say to you, since you look so much like him, but not really, no. No offense, of course. I like his early stuff, and he had an unbelievable voice, but by the time I started paying attention, he was playing to the blue-haired lady set."

Elvis 17 nodded easily and didn't seem offended at all. "Ah know what you mean about those early years. That's why Ah chose to look like this. Ah love doin' *Blue Moon of Kentucky* or *That's Alright, Mama,* but you won't catch me singing *Burnin' Love* or *In the Ghetto.* Ah kind of feel sorry for ole Elvis, to tell you the truth. Ah think he was loyal to the Colonel, and he got trapped between not wanting to hurt him and not wanting to make another movie that was exactly like the last six." He shrugged. "Or, it's possible that Ah have no idea what Ah'm talking about."

I like this guy. I'd have hung out with him. Maybe that could happen. "Listen…I don't know if Buddy and Pertime are gonna find Elvis or not. But either way, I'd love it if you'd come and jam with me tonight. We can do a little of those hillbilly blues, and it'll sound nice. Whaddya say?"

"Jimmy, Ah think that's great. Ah'd be honored. Most people want the real article, not us impersonators, so it means a lot that you'd ask me. Ah'll be there."

Just as 17 said that, Buddy and Pertime came around a corner, laughing but alone. When Jimmy turned back to finish his conversation, 17 was gone. *Doesn't anybody in this place ever just walk away?*

"Hey, Jimmy," Buddy said, "no go on finding Elvis. No one knows where he is."

"I guess he's left the building," Pertime said.

Jimmy gave a half-laugh, mostly-groan and said, "C'mon, let's get out of here. I can't take these bad jokes anymore."

The trio walked under the solid gold portcullis, across the drawbridge and back onto the golden road. All the paving records were Elvis songs. *I'd best not forget that. Whether or not I liked* Spinout *or* Rubberneckin' *is beside the point. Not everyone who bought all these was a blue-haired granny.* Right then, Jimmy's eye caught a gold album called *50,000,000 Elvis Fans Can't Be Wrong.*

"Elvis's castle isn't in the '50s or '60s section. It's kind of its own world," Pertime said. "The '60s are dead ahead."

They turned a bend and saw another town, much bigger than the 1950s section. Psychedelic billboards greeted them, such as a multicolored peace sign that looked like it had been painted by Peter Max. Others had odd images, like a long-haired girl in bell-bottoms, wearing a headband with huge kaleidoscope eyes. As they got closer, Jimmy saw another billboard that showed a rifle with a daisy planted in it and "Make love, not war" scrawled across it.

"Far out, man," Jimmy said.

Chapter Nine

Sitar music floated on the breeze, and Jimmy felt certain he recognized the unforgettable smell of marijuana too. He looked at Pertime. "Am I smelling what I think I am? That sure smells like pot to me."

Pertime shook his head. "No. There are no drugs anywhere in Rock 'n Roll Heaven. Do you remember, as you were finishing your Ascension, how it felt like The Light was everywhere in you, as if it filled you up?"

Jimmy warmed to the memory and smiled. "Yeah. I've never felt anything like that."

"That was His love filling you. It burns out the negative habits and energies you were bringing with you from Earth. Those things do not exist here."

"Okay, that's cool, and it's a much easier way to dry out than going through withdrawal and having DTs, but it doesn't matter one way or the other to me. I gave up all that stuff long ago. There's nothing good down that path for me. If there aren't any drugs here, though, why do I smell dope?"

"It's part of where we are. In the '50s, you probably smelled the fresh-cut grass. That was an innocent time. The '60s turned in another direction, and the scent of marijuana is a part of the fabric of the time. It won't get you high, though. Think of it as incense."

They were on the outskirts of town, and Jimmy saw a number of larger buildings here, some of them rising ten stories or more. "This place looks pretty big. There can't have been enough people playing rock 'n roll in the sixties to fill all these buildings. Are they just props, or do people really live and work here?"

"You're right, there aren't enough musicians to fill this place," Buddy said. "A lot of people that were connected with rock 'n roll never picked up an instrument onstage. Plus, there are the fans. Some people loved the music enough that they were offered entrance into Rock 'n Roll Heaven when they died. Some had the choice between moving on to where He is, or coming here, and they chose to be here. They make up the audience every night."

Makes sense. Playing and singing by yourself is cool, but doing it in front of an appreciative audience is like nothing else. At the same time, I'm not sure I would have chosen it over the chance to stand in that light I felt when I arrived.

He saw that he was in front of the first club he'd seen in the sixties. It wasn't much, just an opening between two nondescript brick buildings that led down a flight of stairs. Above these was a small sign that said *perceptions↓*. Buddy and Pertime looked at Jimmy expectantly, like it was a pop quiz.

"Okay, I can figure this out. Let's see, it's the '60s, so "perceptions" could be just about anybody. This place doesn't look like much, it's not flashy. It looks like one of those beatnik hangouts where everybody sat around and drank coffee, got high and read beat poetry."

Just like that, it fell into place.

"I got it… Aldous Huxley's *The Doors of Perception.* I read it when I was a teenager, because it was the book that inspired Jim Morrison to name *The Doors.* Holy heck, is that right? Is this Jim Morrison's place?"

Buddy smiled and clapped Jimmy on the shoulder, leading him down the stairs to the dirty concrete entrance. Inside, Jimmy smelled fresh coffee brewing, overpowered by the smoke of *cannabis sativa.*

If someone isn't smokin' in the boy's room, they're using a heck of a lot of incense.

The inside was mostly dark, lit only by a few ceiling lights glowing softly behind a tall wooden bar. The walls were unadorned granite. There were a few tables scattered around the room, with white tablecloths that seemed slightly out of place in an otherwise minimalist joint. There was one small stage stuck in a corner, just about big enough to hold two people. It had a single microphone stand.

Slouched at one of the tables sat the Lizard King, Jim Morrison. Not the bloated, drugged-out Jim Morrison of his untimely heart attack in a Paris bathtub. He was once again the Young Lion, with tousled brown hair framing his slate-gray eyes, chiseled cheekbones and full lips. Even leaning sleepily against the table, one leg propped up on a chair, Morrison radiated energy.

"Hello, Per… Buddy. Who's the new guy?" His voice was a smooth baritone with a little bit of lazy twang that betrayed his Texas upbringing.

"Jim, this is Jimmy Velvet. Jimmy, Jim Morrison," Buddy said.

Jimmy stepped forward and stuck out his hand. "Nice to meet you, Jim. I'm a big fan of your work, especially *Crystal Ship.* I used to close my second set with that one for years."

Jimmy's hand hung there, orphaned, for two long heartbeats before Jim let his leg fall to the floor with a clunk and reached out and took Jimmy's hand. A ten-year-old boy's puckish grin tugged at the corner of his mouth. His eyes lit up a little.

"*Crystal Ship,* huh? Wow, you guys must have been a lot of laughs."

"Well," Jimmy said, "to tell you the truth, I did it all those years, trying to figure out what the heck it was about, anyway."

"Is that right?" Jim leaned in conspiratorially. "D'you still want to know?"

"Damned right I do," Jimmy said.

"I can tell you." He looked left and right, as if for spies. Jimmy thought he was about to lift the table cloth up and look underneath it. Finally, he said, "It was about drugs. Every single song I ever wrote is about drugs, right? That's what they said."

Jimmy sighed. *A straight answer isn't in his cards.* He

looked at Jim Morrison—*Jim Morrison!*—and realized why no one had ever been able to stay mad at the guy.

"So, Jim, do you play music in here? The stage looks pretty small. How do you fit a whole band?"

"Nope. No music in *perceptions.* In fact, I haven't sung a note since I climbed in that damned bathtub in Paris, fell asleep and woke up on that shore where everything is quiet. We just do poetry here, man."

Jimmy couldn't tell if the "man" was a lingering hangover of the sixties, or if Jim was putting him on. No one ever knew when he was serious in life. Nothing's changed.

"When everybody gets tired of rotting their brains out with music, and they're looking for a little conversation or introspection, they come here. *perceptions* is a refuge from the endless chaos of Heaven. Who ever knew you would need such a thing?"

"Are you still writing poetry, then?"

"That's the damnedest thing, isn't it? I had a bunch of projects started that I would love to finish. I get fresh ideas in my head all the time, and I try to follow them, but I get lost. I haven't written a single word since I got here. No one has. There isn't any new music, or poetry. In fact, there's no new art of any kind here. It's just a lot of mental masturbation, now. Same shit, different plane."

Jimmy looked at Buddy, who was a prolific songwriter, with more than forty songs to his name by the time he turned twenty-two.

"How 'bout you, Buddy? You've been here a long time, now. Written anything?"

"Nothin', Jimmy." Buddy looked at the ground, took a deep breath, then looked at Jimmy again. "Jim's right. No one's ever written anything new here. We can all remember every single bit of our own songs, and we can all learn each other's songs if we didn't already know them, but we can't write anything new."

Jimmy let out a long, low whistle. "But… why? Everyone

here is a creative soul. Why would something stop you from creating?"

"No one knows," Buddy said, "but it's true. Once in a while word will spread that someone has written something new, but it always turns out to be a song that they had heard from someone else here and thought they were writing themselves. Sometimes, I feel like it's so close. An idea comes and it feels like it's going to come together, then...nothing."

"That big guy with the long white beard doesn't tell you that, does he, Jimmy?" Jim said. "Did he give you the same routine he gave me?" He lowered his voice, moving his chin against his chest in a decent impersonation of the Big Guy, whom Jimmy had about decided must be St. Peter. "SON, I HAVE A CHOICE FOR YOU, AND MIGHT I SAY, THAT'S SOMETHING A LOT OF PEOPLE WHO ARE IN YOUR POSITION WOULD LIKE TO HAVE..."

Jimmy laughed, just a little. Pertime glanced around uncomfortably, smirked, then wiped it away.

"Well, I'll tell you," Jim went on, "That's a crock. Sitting here doing nothing but going over the old words seems like it'll be better than being in that other place, but some days I'm not so sure..." He trailed off and let his eyes focus in the distance, lost in his own thoughts.

Buddy Holly walked over and laid a hand on Jim Morrison's arm. It was exceedingly odd to Jimmy's eye to see the icons of two very different generations of rock 'n roll standing side by side. "It's not that bad, Jim," Buddy said. His voice was low. Gentle.

Jim snapped out of his reverie, looked up and smiled a bit of the impish grin at Buddy. "I suppose. Some days just seem to last forever, you know? I was pretty burned out toward the end, when Pam and I were in Paris, but now…now I feel recharged, but there's no way for me to let out the words that build up inside me." He shook his head in frustration.

Pertime cleared his throat. Buddy said, "Come on guys, we better keep movin'. As long as the days are around here, we've still got a schedule to keep. I don't want to have to fill out all the forms to lengthen the day again."

Jim stood up, stretched like a panther awakened from a nap and said: "Jimmy, it's nice to meet you. Seriously it is, no shit. I'll be there at your show tonight."

"If you're going to be there anyway, you don't want to come up on stage and do *Crystal Ship* with me, do you? That would be the coolest."

Jim Morrison looked at him without saying anything for four beats…five. His cool demeanor returned, and he shook his head before sinking back down into the chair and looking away.

Buddy, Pertime and Jimmy let themselves out the same way they came in.

Chapter Ten

It was still fully light outside. Maybe Jim Morrison was right, and the days really did last forever here.

They climbed the stairs up out of the cellar and stepped back onto the golden road. Pertime and Buddy led Jimmy further on into the sixties section of Rock 'n Roll Heaven, past other clubs big and small. They all looked dark and closed up. In most cases, Jimmy knew instantly who belonged to which club. *Mama's Place* had to belong to Cass Elliott. *Canned Heat Blues?* Bob Hite or Alan Wilson. Now and then, he had to ask his guides. When they walked by *Hamlet,* which looked like a typical '60s nightclub, Jimmy couldn't make any connection to a combined Shakespeare buff and rock 'n roller.

"*Hamlet* belongs to Richard Manuel, from The Band," Pertime said. "He named it after the dog he had when he lived up at Big Pink with Bob Dylan and the rest of The Band."

"To be, or not to be…" Jimmy left it at that.

The next mystery was a huge grass hut with a wooden sign out front: *Neptune's Cocktail*. Jimmy puzzled over it for a few moments but gave up. "That's Dennis Wilson's place," said Pertime. "I don't know what a Neptune's cocktail is, but it won't get you drunk, since it's here."

Buddy said with a wink: "But if anyone was gonna figure out how to make booze around here, it just might be Dennis. Let's go ask him."

"Is he there?" Jimmy asked. "Man, I loved the Beach Boys."

"Only one way to find out," Buddy said.

They stepped off the golden road and immediately onto sand, which flowed all the way inside the hut. It was light outside, but murky inside, lit only by tiki torches.

Behind the bar was man with a bushy beard and long, unkempt hair. He wore an unbuttoned shirt and board shorts, feet bare. Sitting on a stool across the counter was a black man in slacks and a subdued herringbone sport coat. "This is Dennis Wilson and Sam Cooke," said Buddy. "Boys, this is Jimmy Velvet."

Dennis Wilson came out from behind the bar with athletic grace, and he and Sam Cooke both shook Jimmy's hand. Dennis said, "Welcome to the land of the non-living. I'd offer you a drink, but there is no such thing here. We do our best without it."

Jimmy smiled and said, "I don't think I'll ever get used to this. Meeting you both is something special."

Buddy leaned in and said, "We're taking Jimmy on the tour. He asked us why you call your place *Neptune's Cocktail*, and we had to admit that we don't know."

"Yeah, well, it's a surfer term. When you've surfed for a while, you learn that when you're going to wipe out, you hold your breath so you don't swallow a bunch of salt water. Before you figure that out, though, you end up with a belly full of ocean—Neptune's Cocktail. When I first got here, I felt a lot like I didn't belong, so I thought that was a fitting name."

"*You* don't feel like you belong! You were a Beach Boy," Jimmy said. He turned to Sam. "...and you were one of the greatest singers and songwriters of all time. I had a bootleg copy of a concert you did that I listened to all the time. How could either of you feel out of place?"

"It's like this," Dennis said. "If I had led exactly the same life, but had picked up garbage for a living instead of beating on the drums and singing with my brothers, where would I be? We all know where I would be, and..." He stopped and looked away for a moment. "I just don't know that it's right that I'm here, instead of there."

No one knew what to say.

"I didn't mean to harsh everybody's mood," Dennis said,

smiling again, though it didn't quite reach his eyes.

Everyone laughed a little and Jimmy looked around. *Neptune's* had a long bar, patio-style tables and chairs, and a low stage with a drum set right up front, along with keyboards, guitars, amps and monitors. At the far end, an oversized hammock swayed as if in a gentle breeze.

"I know it's a lot to ask, Dennis," Jimmy said, "but I don't have a drummer for my first show tonight, and I was wondering if you would mind sitting in with me?"

"Well, that depends. What kind of music are you gonna play? These days, I just play what I want."

"I've always been a rock 'n roller, so that's what it'll be tonight. We'll be doing stuff from the late fifties up through the seventies. I never did care too much for the stuff that came later, all those synthesizers and electronic drums…"

"Well, it ain't no thing, if it don't got that swing…you've got yourself a drummer."

Jimmy smiled. *Exactly what every drummer I ever knew said.* He turned to Sam Cooke. "I don't have my set list put together yet, but I definitely know I want to do *A Change is Gonna Come.* I've sung that song since I was just starting out, but I wonder…if we play it, will you sing it for me?"

"I think maybe that's a good one for tonight. I'll be there. I'll sing it, if that's what you want."

"That is definitely what I want," Jimmy said.

"We've got to keep moving, Jimmy," Pertime said, leading him toward the door, "or we're never going to get you where you need to be."

"Okay. I'll see you guys tonight," Jimmy waved as they left. Just ahead, the Golden Road made a Y around the biggest building they had come across since Elvis's castle. Other than its size, which would have covered two or three city blocks, it looked like it belonged at the side of a dusty Texas highway. It had weather-beaten wooden siding, a porch that stretched as far as Jimmy could see, and a set of horns hanging over the door that could have belonged to Babe the Blue Ox. Above it all was a neon sign that said *Pearl's Big O*. Beneath that was a pearl with a feminine face, lipsticked lips rounded in an 'Oh!'

"I like it, but I'm at a loss. No idea whose place that could be."

"Well, that's a new place that's just gone up. Roy Orbison's place used to be on that side of the street," Buddy nodded to the right, "and Janis Joplin's place was on the other side. A little while ago, they decided to put their places together, and so *Pearl's* and *The Big O's* became *Pearl's Big O*."

That set Jimmy back. *Janis Joplin and Roy Orbison...together. I have trouble picturing this.*

Buddy said, "We may not be able to make new music here, but some things can't be stopped, and the heart wants what the heart wants. Roy and Janis, well, they wanted to be together, so they are."

"Lucky Roy."

"I see some lights on in there," Buddy said. "You wanna go meet them, see what they're up to?"

"Do I want to meet Roy Orbison and Janis Joplin?" Jimmy laughed. "Yes. Yes, I do."

The closer they got to the front entrance, the more overwhelming its size felt. Up close, the front doors looked twelve feet high. Buddy pushed on them; they swung open with ease.

The inside was just as impressive. Along the entire left side ran a polished bar with a mirror behind it. At the back stood a stage that looked large enough to hold ten bands at once. The rest was one big dance floor with real wood floors and sawdust spread around. Jimmy closed his eyes. *I can imagine several thousand people in here, moving to the rhythm of the music. If I get my own place, as I'm told I do, I could do a lot worse than this.*

From the back of the stage came an amplified voice...*the* voice. No one but Roy Orbison. "Hey, Per? Is that you? We're still working out the acoustics since the big changeover. Can you hang on a minute? We'll be right down."

Roy stepped to the mic stand at the front of the stage. He was wearing a black shirt, black slacks, boots and dark Wayfarer sunglasses. His dark hair was pushed back in his '60s style, rather than the shaggy bangs and ponytail he had favored in later years. He nodded toward stage left. Four men wandered out, picked up their instruments and began to play. Jimmy was hoping to hear *In Dreams*, or *Crying*, but it was *Piece of My Heart*. Instead of Janis's bluesy shout, Roy stepped to the microphone and let his honeyed tenor fly on the intro.

Strain as he might, Jimmy couldn't recognize any of the players behind Roy. Whoever they were, they were tighter than Big Brother and the Holding Company ever dreamed of being. After a few bars, a woman in her mid-twenties wandered on the stage, laughing and making obscene gestures to the band. Her wavy dishwater blonde hair fell halfway down her back, woven through with blue and yellow feathers. She wore a colorful peasant blouse, star-spangled bell bottoms, and round, rose-colored sunglasses pushed halfway down her nose.

When Roy was midway through the first verse, she sidled up and hugged him. The two guitarists shared a microphone on the side, providing the buildup to the famous chorus. Together, Roy and Janis leaned into the mic at center stage and cut loose.

Roy Orbison had one of the greatest voices in the history of rock 'n roll. Janis was known for her soul and willingness to shred her vocal cords in the service of the blues. Individually, they were legends. Together, they were a miracle.

Janis sang her signature song just as she always did, while Roy soared above and around her voice, his sweet tenor filling in every gap. Without thought, Jimmy's feet carried him toward the stage, a smile spreading across his face. When he got close, he stood in rapt attention.

Halfway through the song, Roy moved away and nodded at Janis. She didn't miss a beat. Roy walked to the wings and conferred with an older man carrying a clipboard, taking notes. When Janis came to the end of the final run-through of the chorus, she placed her feet wide apart, threw her head back and cut loose with a wail that sent chills down Jimmy's spine. He felt like she was reaching out directly to grab his soul. For the first time in Rock 'n Roll Heaven, Jimmy felt tears well up and spill down his cheeks.

The band played the final bars of the song and looked at Janis. "Take a break, boys, I think we've just about got 'er," she said. Her whiskey-fueled twang hadn't changed a bit. She leaned back into the microphone and said, "Who you bringing around now, Pertime? Who's the lucky deader?" Her hoarse laugh reminded Jimmy of a schoolgirl with a precocious smoking habit. He turned to see Pertime standing right beside him.

"Janis, this is Jimmy Velvet, our newest arrival. Jimmy, this is Janis and Roy."

"Believe me, no introductions are necessary." Jimmy wiped the back of his arm across the back of his eyes. "That was…can't describe it. I never would have dreamed that…" Jimmy paused, not wanting to offend.

"What," Roy said, walking down the stage front stairs, "that our voices would sound like that together? We didn't know either, but we get some pretty interesting jam sessions here, as you might imagine. One night, I wandered into *Pearl's,* Janis invited me up on stage and…" He reached out and took her hand. "…magic."

They're glowing. It's good to see that someone's happy here. After Jim Morrison and Dennis Wilson, I was wondering. "I'd sure be glad to hear more music like that. Are you guys going to sing together all the time?"

"Yes sir, all the time," Roy said. "Or at least as long as she'll share the stage with me. You're welcome to stop by any time. Tonight, though, we'll be at your place."

"That's freaking me out a little bit, to be truthful," Jimmy said. "I've never had stage fright in my life, but I'm already feeling it."

Janis stepped close to Jimmy, put an arm around him and hugged him quickly. "Nothin' to worry about. We're all just musicians for the love of it. You'll never find a better crowd than you'll have tonight. It'll be fine."

"Once you play that first riff, it'll be just like any other gig," Buddy said. *Says you, Buddy Holly. I've been lucky to play in front of fifty people a night these past years, and none of them were named Roy Orbison or Janis Joplin.*

"Uh, Janis, Roy." Jimmy said. "I've got guitarists and my drummer covered, but I'm wondering if you guys would help me out with vocals. Not meaning to suggest you're backup si—"

"Slow down, sugar," Janis said. "We've checked our egos at the door. Dying will do that for you, or at least it did for me. We'll be glad to be there, won't we, hon?"

"You bet," Roy said. His face suggested a mischievous look behind the Wayfarers. "We wouldn't miss it. We've heard you're 'the one.'"

"'The one what?'" Jimmy asked, his voice rising an octave.

"Roy!" Janis exclaimed. "I was just gettin' this boy settled down and then you've gotta put all that on him?" She turned to Jimmy and said, "Never you mind about all that. Some people like to see ghosts where there aren't none and *some people* aren't happy unless they're looking for a savior. You just be yourself and play your music and you'll be fine. We'll be there to help out."

Roy nodded his approval, looked contrite. Jimmy smiled nervously. He'd never done well under pressure. *Whatever this 'The One' shit is, I'm already nervous enough without it. If someone's going to be the savior in Rock 'n Roll Heaven, it'll be Buddy Holly or Elvis Presley, not Jimmy Velvet.*

Chapter Eleven

Jimmy glanced down at the records passing under his feet and saw that they had left the sixties behind. He saw a gold record for *The Locomotion,* but it was by Grand Funk, not Little Eva. He saw *Mr. Blue Sky*, by Electric Light Orchestra, *Stuck in the Middle* by Stealers Wheel and *The Year of the Cat* by Al Stewart.

"I keep calling this place 'Rock 'n Roll Heaven,' but it's not really, is it?" Jimmy asked. "I mean, I met Sam Cooke back there. I know how lucky I am to meet him. He was one of the greatest performers ever, but he wasn't exactly rock 'n roll."

"That's part of the design," Pertime said. "Remember, this place hasn't always been called that. When Buddy, Ritchie and J.P. arrived, the place didn't have a name. It just was. Only more recently, people started giving it a name. It's stuck, even with the angels, because it sounds better than 'That Place Where All the People Who Made Popular Music Live.' That's not very catchy."

Jimmy smiled and looked up at the billboards welcoming them to the seventies. One side of the road had a large sign that said, *Keep on Truckin': Welcome to The Seventies – Music's Greatest Decade*. A little further on, a smaller sign read *Can you dig it?* in overstuffed balloon letters. The smell of marijuana now mixed with stuff like patchouli, oolong tea, and incense.

I feel right at home.

The buildings ahead reached for the skies, with mirrored glass windows and odd shapes. He even saw a round building that looked like stacks of albums, similar to the Capitol Records building in Los Angeles. The golden road, which had started out as a small, winding path leading into the fifties, spread out into a broad four-lane thoroughfare.

"Were there so many people making music in the seventies that they needed all this space?" Jimmy marveled.

"Partially, yes," Pertime said. "But it's more than that."

"Rock 'n roll changed from the time when I played it," Buddy said. "When I started, everything was natural, organic. Almost a mom and pop operation. Look at what one man, Sam Phillips, was able to do with Sun Studios. He put out records by Elvis Presley, Jerry Lee Lewis, Roy Orbison, Johnny Cash, Howlin' Wolf and Carl Perkins. That got harder as the industry matured. Things started to evolve in the sixties, and then sped up and went corporate in the seventies. The landscape here reflects that. The business might have changed, but people stayed the same…" Buddy nodded his head to a small group on a sidewalk up ahead.

Two men and a woman were singing, each man playing an acoustic guitar. Jimmy changed course and walked toward them. From a block away he recognized Jim Croce and Cass Elliot. Closer still, he saw that the second man was Harry Chapin. A trio for the ages, but there was no crowd around them. No one else noticed them.

When he got within earshot, Jimmy immediately recognized their song: *Where Have All the Flowers Gone?*. Cass's gorgeous voice sang lead, with Jim and Harry harmonizing beneath her. They appeared lost in their music and the blending of their voices. After that song, Jim Croce began strumming *Blowing in the Wind*, with his companions joining in three-part harmony. "Do little concerts like that break out all the time?" Jimmy asked.

Pertime shrugged. "It happens. The days can be long, so musicians often find other like-minded people and teach each other songs, or new instruments, or new techniques."

"It's been one of the best things about this place for me," Buddy said. "The style of guitar playing was a lot simpler when I was doing it. Some of these guys have really jazzed it up. I still like what we did; it was straightforward and honest—but learning new things is a great way to pass the time."

"By the way," Pertime interrupted. "There's someone up ahead I think you're really going to want to see, Jimmy."

Jimmy laughed and said, "I've met Buddy Holly, Jim Morrison, Roy Orbison and Janis Joplin, just to name a few. I can't imagine anybody else that's gonna knock my socks off any more than that."

"Heroes and legends are one thing," Buddy said, "but perspective is everything."

"I have no idea what that means, but okay."

In between the tall buildings stood smaller individual clubs. One nearby had a glittering neon sign that flashed *Killer* at the top and *Queen* at the bottom.

"Freddie Mercury?"

"Of course," said Pertime, as if any fool should know that.

Directly across from *Killer Queen* was a smaller building with a sign that read *Kath's Klub*. Underneath was a hand-lettered sign: *All guitar gods welcome*. Jimmy's eyebrows shot up. "Terry Kath! That guy was awesome. I remember Chicago came and played at the McNeil Penitentiary in the early seventies. I wanted to go see them, but not badly enough to go to McNeil Island. He was incredible, but never got the credit he deserved for his guitar work."

"He doesn't do concerts, really," Buddy said. "He just lets people bring their guitars and hang out. I've played in some jams there that went on and on. We did a version of *Sugar Magnolia* that lasted for days. Do you know that song?"

"We used to jam on it in the Velvets when we were burned out from too many shows in a row." They walked past *Allman Joys*, Duane Allman's club, then *That Smell,* Ronnie Van Zant's place, right next door to each other. "I think I could live here forever and not get to see everyone I want," Jimmy said.

"It seems that way, doesn't it?" Buddy answered, "but forever is a really long time. Even the little slice of forever I've seen has started to wear me down a little."

As they walked, they left the busiest part of town and the

buildings got smaller again. Ahead, a sign said *In the Pocket*, with an animated 8-ball dropping over and over into a pool table corner pocket. "Bet that belongs to a bass player," said Jimmy. "They're always talking about staying in the pocket."

"You are correct," Pertime answered. "That's our next stop."

In the Pocket looked like a small-town neighborhood bar. It was one story, painted red, with blacked-out windows filled with neon beer signs advertising Rhinelander, Schlitz, and Budweiser beer. The heavy oak door opened into a dark, space that smelled of deep-fried food and chalk dust. There were a few tall tables, designed so you could lean on them without sitting down, scattered around three standard pool tables, a bumper pool table, a shuffleboard table and two dart boards. A small stage sat off to one side at the very back of the room. Pertime said, "There are some people back there you're going to want to see. We'll wait here. No introductions will be required."

A man sat at the very back of the room, facing the stage, perhaps lost in his own thoughts. Jimmy walked toward him, bumping into a chair that scraped against the floor, startling the man. He turned to look at the noise. Jimmy hadn't seen the face in two decades, but he knew it like a brother's.

"Jon!"

Jon Averill jumped to his feet and dashed over, grabbing Jimmy in a long embrace, pounding him on the back.

"Jimmy! I knew I'd see you here some day. It's so good to see you, man. But what happened? You got old. Is that grey hair? I thought we were all supposed to die before we got old."

"I probably should have...don't know how I lasted as long as I did. It's good to see you, man."

Jon's smile faded. "You too, Jimmy. I don't know how long it seems to you since we've seen each other, but for me it's been a hundred lifetimes. Time refuses to pass here. It should be great—we're given everything we ever wanted and can do anything we want except get drunk or stoned, but..." His voice trailed off.

"But, what, Jon? This should be the best thing that ever happened to us. It's a chance to see the greatest players of all time every night, and we can sit down and jam any time we want. What could be bad about that?"

"It is great. At first. I couldn't believe I could go see Otis Redding one night, then Johnny Burnette the next and catch Gram Parsons the next. I felt like every night was that first night when The Beatles appeared on the Ed Sullivan show. After a while, though, it got old. No new songs, just all of us playing the same old stuff, over and over. It's like Ricky Nelson said in *Garden Party*: if I only get to play the same songs over and over, I'd just as soon drive a truck."

Jimmy nodded, reached out and put his arm around his old friend. "I get it. I just don't know what can be done about it, unless you know where a back door is that leads back to the good ol' USA."

"Well," Jon said, "everyone's all excited about you, for some reason. They all think you're The One, and that you're going to change things here." He shrugged. "I guess that's possible…"

"…but not likely," Jimmy agreed. They both laughed at how ludicrous the idea was.

At that moment, a man entered from a back door and came their way. He looked thirtyish, with an old fifties-style brush cut. He was wearing a plain white T-shirt and old jeans rolled up at the cuffs. Something about him tickled the farthest recesses of Jimmy's memory. He stopped a few feet away and smiled.

"Jimmy? Is that you? By God, you look just like your dad."

"Uncle Billy?" Jimmy's throat closed a little. Tears formed but didn't fall.

"The one and only," Bill said. "I'd ask you how you're doing, but I'm going to guess this trip started with a really bad day and has only gotten weirder from there."

Jimmy reached out and hugged him tight. He smelled the same, a combination of Brylcreem and Old Spice. It took Jimmy back to his childhood.

"You gave me my first guitar and taught me my first chords. Mom always blamed you for…"

"Your mom blamed me for just about everything other than rain and snow," Bill interrupted. "But that was all right. I knew where she was coming from. I don't blame her."

Jimmy laughed. "She thought you were a bad influence on me. She wanted me to turn out more like Dad than you, but the music got into me and had to find a way out."

This is the hardest part to take in. Outside of Rollie, in all The Black Velvets' incarnations, he'd been closest to Jon. They were musical twins–hated the same people, worshipped the same musical gods. Then, Uncle Bill. *Family. I thought I had left that behind forever. It matters more than I imagined.* A sense of belonging, of contentment, washed over him.

"Uncle Billy, you died in that car crash in Mississippi in late '59. Why aren't you back in the fifties part of Rock 'n Roll Heaven?"

"I am. You just missed me when you came through town. You stuck to the Golden Road, right? There's a whole bunch of Rock 'n Roll Heaven off the side paths. Some of the guys I used to play with in bars and I got together, and we've got a little community there. Like Jon said, it feels like I've been here an eternity already, but it hasn't been so bad for us. People keep bringing in new music and styles for me to learn. I spent a long time learning how to play slide guitar from Duane Allman. You never know what's going to pop up next. Anyway, word travels fast around here when there's a new arrival, so I knew you were going to be passing through. I didn't know who 'Jimmy Velvet' was…"

He probably thinks it's dumbass.

"…but I saw you walk by with Pertime and Buddy and recognized you immediately. While you've been killing time meeting everybody, I've been waiting for you here. Jon and I have been buddies for years. I just never connected the Jimmy he was talking about with you, until this morning."

Jimmy hesitated. "You… you haven't seen Dad, have you?"

Bill smiled a little but shook his head. "No. He's dead, huh? I've never seen him or anyone else from the family. You never knew it about your old man, but he played guitar when he was younger, too. We had a nice little trio going, but he gave it up and went to work when Mary got pregnant with the little bundle of joy that grew up to be Jimmy Velvet. Since I hadn't seen him, I was hoping he was still alive."

"He died years ago," Jimmy said. "Heart attack."

Pertime appeared beside Jimmy and laid a hand on his shoulder. "I know they are important to you, Jimmy, but we need to go…"

"I know, I know," Jimmy said. "I'll have plenty of chances to see them later." He turned back to Jon and Bill. "I guess I'm having my opening night, tonight. Will you guys come, hang out on stage with me?" He looked at Bill. "We can do *So Lonesome I Could Cry*, since that was the first song you taught me."

"Sounds good. I'll be there, Jimmy."

"Jon, do you still remember *Rock 'n Roll Boogaloo?* I haven't done that song since you… left. It didn't feel right playing it without you. I'd love to do it with you tonight."

Jon gave Jimmy a quick embrace. "You got it, brother. I still remember it."

As soon as they were outside *In the Pocket,* Jimmy stopped.

"Fellas, we can stop right here. I don't need to go any farther. This is where my home is. Buddy, I loved your music and I can't wait to play more of it, but '50s music was just a foundation for me. In some ways, the music of the '60s was the greatest music of all time, but I was still a kid then. For me, it's always been about the '70s. This is my home."

"Are you sure?" Pertime said. "We've still got more ground to cover. Steve Marriott's place is up ahead, and Bob Marley, too. There's still the eighties ahead. There aren't too many people there yet, but it will fill up over time."

Jimmy shook his head. "There was some good music in the eighties, but the rock 'n roll seemed to be more about hairspray, eyeliner and crotch rock than great music. I belong right here."

Pertime and Buddy exchanged a glance, and Pertime said, "All right, if that's what you want. We've got room for your place just up ahead here. Come on."

Jimmy's step quickened now. After just a few minutes, they stopped in front of a nondescript gray building. The most distinguishing feature about the building was its lack of distinguishing features.

Crap. I should have known.

"Yeah, I guess that's about right. I never accomplished much, so this fits."

Buddy laughed, but just a little. "You're gonna have to work harder than that to be disappointed. This is the way everybody's place looks in the beginning. Let's go inside."

They opened the plain grey door and were greeted by more dull sameness as far as the eye could see. The only feature in the entire building was a small wooden table with two chairs. In one sat an elderly man in a dapper, charcoal-gray three-piece business suit.

Chapter Twelve

"Jimmy, this is Frank," Pertime said, indicating the man in the business suit. "Frank, please meet Jimmy Velvet. This is going to be his place."

The man at the table had a receding hairline, white hair swept straight back. A bit jowly, but with alert dark eyes. He rose and extended his hand. "A pleasure to meet you. I'll be the architect of your new home. Sit down, please."

Both took seats. Frank picked up a large sketch pad. "Tell me what you have in mind. The only limit is your imagination. It can help to close your eyes."

Jimmy leaned back in the chair and let his mind wander. *Where do I start?* He thought about all the other places he had seen in Rock 'n Roll Heaven—the down-home comfort of Buddy's skating rink, the epic grandeur of Elvis's castle, how perfectly appropriate Bobby Darin's nightclub, Dennis Wilson's beach hut and Jon Averill's neighborhood pool hall had been.

Then everything fell into place.

"I want my place to be called *Jimmy's Real Rock 'n Roll*, with a sign outside in the shape of a my Stratocaster that says that. I don't want the place to be too big, but I want enough room for everyone that wants to be able to come and have a good time. I'd like it to remind me a bit of the dives I always played, but maybe a little nicer and definitely a little cleaner. I want a big stage with room for any of my friends that want to come and play. I want a sound system that can be heard all the way to the rest of heaven, because rock 'n roll should be played loud."

Frank sat listening to Jimmy, watching him, before he put his pencil to the sketch pad and started to draw.

"There has to be a big dance floor right in front of the stage, because we will get people dancing. Guaranteed." Jimmy closed his eyes for a moment. When he opened them again, they were alight with passion. "There's got to be a big Wurlitzer jukebox over there in the corner," he said, pointing, "that I want to stock with all the records from the Golden Road. I know there's no alcohol here, but I still want the signs, because it won't look right without them. We'll need neon signs for Mickey's Big Mouths, Milwaukee's Best, Olympia, Rainier, and Bud, but no light beer signs. There's got to be a kitchen in the back that makes bar food like burgers and nachos and wings, so we'll need tables scattered around the rest of the place. They don't need to be fancy, but they should all have red-checked plastic tablecloths on them, and every one should have a bowl of peanuts in the middle that never runs out."

Now Frank's fingers flew across the page. As they did, the room began to swirl and change. *Jimmy's Real Rock 'n Roll* began to take shape. The stage came into focus, with a drum riser in the back and stacks of Marshall amps lining both sides. A brightly-lit rainbow jukebox appeared where none had been a minute earlier.

Jimmy saw none of it. His eyes were closed again, describing what was in his head.

"The floorboards need to be wood, but smooth, so people can dance. I want fans overhead, too, and bathrooms that are always clean. What I'd really like," Jimmy said, eyes still closed, smiling widely, "is a dressing room. I got so tired of getting ready to play behind a wall that doesn't even have a place to sit. I'd really love a dressing room with a mirror and a chair so I can tune my guitar before I go on."

Jimmy went quiet, but Frank's pencil still whipped across the page, sketching the reality that shaped around them. After a few moments, Frank put his pencil down and blew the stray graphite dust off the page.

Jimmy Velvet opened his eyes to see everything he had envisioned. He could only look around and gawk, struck mute.

Frank stood up, took one lingering look at his creation, then folded shut the cover of the notebook and slipped it into a portfolio. He put out his hand to Jimmy again. "It was a pleasure. I think you'll like what I made for you here, son. I do. Enjoy it."

Jimmy took his hand in both of his. "Sir, this is like the inside of my brain come to life. I can't thank you enough. Would you like to come to our first show tonight?"

"Thank you, young man, but no. My idea of great music is a Beethoven Sonata. Enjoy your place."

Frank walked out a back door that Jimmy swore hadn't been there a moment before, and was gone.

Jimmy did a complete 360-degree turn, absorbing all the elements of his new home in disbelief. "So this is really mine?"

"Yep," Buddy said. "Take a look at that sign outside, if you want. It's all yours."

"One more order of business, now," Pertime said. He traced a rectangle on a table and Jimmy saw his own reflection looking back up at him. Pertime put his finger in the lower right hand corner of the rectangle and moved it slowly to the left. As he did, the image of Jimmy changed. The salt and pepper in his hair gave way to the original dark brown. The crow's feet and laugh lines in his face faded. "It's time to pick what age you will be in Rock 'n Roll Heaven. No matter what shell you choose, your spirit and knowledge will be the same. Take your time, scroll back and forth, check yourself out. It's a big decision."

Jimmy turned a chair around and sat down backwards, his chin resting on his fist. He reached out idly, flicking the bottom of the image left and right, watching himself get younger, then older. After a few moments, he sighed and pushed the image as far to the right as it would go.

"I earned these lines, these gray hairs. They mean something to me. I'll stay just like I am."

Pertime smiled gently. "Being who you are is always a good choice. That's everything, then. This is the end of the tour.

You're on your own now. I've enjoyed seeing Rock 'n Roll Heaven through your eyes."

"Can you come to my opening night? It's gonna be an epically good time."

Pertime shook his head, not unkindly. "This is a place made for humans, not angels. We only come here on official business."

"Will I see you again?"

"Heaven is forever, so is the soul. I never know what tomorrow will bring, but I am often sent to Rock 'n Roll Heaven. Other angels think it smells bad here."

"I'm going to miss you, Pertime. I don't know what angel protocol is, but..." Jimmy threw his arms around Pertime, buried his face in his shoulder and said, "Thank you."

A moment later, Jimmy was holding air.

He was alone with Buddy, who was looking outside the window. "It's starting to get dark. Good. Per is right. Rock 'n roll should never be played in the daytime. Let's take a look at what you've got going on here."

They walked over to the stage and stepped up and looked out over the house.

"Rock 'n Roll Heaven is a big place, Buddy. If even a tiny fraction of everyone shows up, we'll never fit them in here. We can hold what, 200, 250 people in here?"

"No need to worry. It doesn't work like that here. We can fit as many people as we need to and you'll never notice a thing. It's bigger on the inside than it is on the outside."

"I'll take your word for it. How about everybody's instruments? Your guitars, Dennis' drums, Jon's bass? I asked a lot of singers too, so we're going to need a lot of microphones."

Buddy reached out and laid a hand on Jimmy's shoulder. "It'll all be taken care of. We'll have everything we need. We always do. Just like in our old lives, there are roadies who will get the stage ready. Let's check out your dressing room."

They walked backstage, then through a black curtain into a large room. Jimmy forgot his worries.

Scattered around the room was every guitar Jimmy had ever owned, from that first Epiphone from Uncle Billy, to the Strat that should have been on the bottom of the Lashton River, along with every other guitar he'd ever called his own. He walked straight to the Epiphone and picked it up, turning it to catch the overhead light. It wasn't just the same model, it was the same guitar, down to the scratches and wear marks he remembered better than his own reflection. He had held on to that guitar his whole life, waiting for the day he could give it to Emily. Now it was here.

He walked along the guitars, brushing his fingers against the Gretsch hollow-body that had been stolen from backstage in 1984 while he was playing a rundown dump just outside Tumwater, Washington. He knelt in front of his Martin 12-string, which he'd been forced to sell when the Magic Bus had needed a new transmission in Bend, Oregon. He hadn't seen it in more than a dozen years, but here it was, looking exactly like it had the night he had let it go.

Finally, he picked up his black sunburst Fender Stratocaster. The strap was already attached, with "Jimmy Velvet" hand-worked into the leather. As soon as he touched it, Jimmy knew that it wasn't a replica. It was the real deal. He slipped it on and strummed a chord; perfect tune. He looked at Buddy, smiling like a birthday boy.

Buddy was nodding. Jimmy thought back to the Gibson J-45 that he had seen leaning up against the hay bales in Buddy's place, the one with "Texas" on the cover. *He understands*. "I knew this would be waiting for you, but I thought it would be better if you saw them for yourself. I know I felt like I'd left part of myself behind until I got my guitars. That's when I knew everything would be all right."

"My only problem is that I want to play them all at the same time," Jimmy said, casting his gaze at the twenty-three different guitars in stands or cases around the room. He slipped the Strat's strap off, picked up the Epiphone and sat down at one of the two straight-backed chairs at the small table, strumming the intro to *Rock 'n Roll Boogaloo,* written with Jon Averill in a cramped backstage area so many years ago and a universe away.

The table was bare except for a single lamp that cast a small pool of light, and a pen laying across a stack of blank pages. Jimmy looked up at Buddy. "C'mon, let's write a song. We can play it tonight. It might not be very tight, but I bet we can figure it out. I don't know if I'm ever going to get a chance like this again. What do you say?"

Buddy shook his head a little. "I can't. Songs and ideas were always coming to me before I died, but now—every time I start to write, it evaporates."

Jimmy took a sheet off the stack, uncapped the pen and looked thoughtfully into space for eight, nine, ten seconds. Then he started to scribble across the top of the page. He held it up to Buddy, a proud kindergartner showing off his ABCs to a parent.

In Jimmy's distinctive, left-slanting handwriting were the words *Edge of Heaven*. He raised his eyebrows at Buddy as if to say, "See? This isn't so hard!"

Buddy's eyes widened a bit. He began to smile.

"I get the idea that people are waiting for a savior here, which is a little odd in a place called Heaven. I'm nothing special. Never have been. What I do have, though, is a great idea for a song. Look!" He slapped the paper down on the table, scribbled for a minute, paused, scratched out a few words and wrote a replacement phrase. He held it out to Buddy.

"Standing on a stage close to heaven
My heart on my sleeve
My guitar in my hand
Cheers ring so loud
From the colossal crowd
But when the curtain goes up
Will they hear what I play?"

He looked at Jimmy with wonder. "This is new? You hadn't written it before you got here?"

"Brand new. Dead honest." *I keep saying that sort of thing while forgetting where I am. People are going to think I should be sent to Wiseass Heaven.*

Buddy squeezed his eyes shut and kept them that way for a long time. "It really is you, then. It's everything about you. You never made it big, but you never burned out. You never turned your back on the music. You got caught up in a lot of the bad stuff that stopped so many people, but you beat it before you got here. No matter what else, for you, it was always about rock 'n roll."

With a slight tremor in his hand, he reached out and took the pen from Jimmy. Buddy leaned over the table, and underneath the last line, wrote:

When the curtain goes up
Will I hear what I say?

Buddy Holly's voice was quiet, sober, and Southern. "May Ah please borra one of your guitars?"

"Any one that suits you. Take your pick."

He grabbed a Guild F-50 six-string Jimmy had owned for a few years in the late seventies. "What do you think of this?"

Buddy adjusted the strap, got the instrument into position, and played a riff. *That's classic Buddy Holly guitar work: a little rockabilly, but melded with a bluesy style he must have picked up when he was jamming with some of the later arrivals.* He played it again, tweaking a few spots on the second run through. Buddy's eyes were closed, but his smile was as wide as Texas. He played the riff again, faster this time, nodding to Jimmy to play along.

Time sped up and flowed around them.

It was done.

A new song was written.

Rock 'n Roll Heaven would never be the same.

Chapter Thirteen

After Jimmy and Buddy finished writing *Edge of Heaven*, they ran through it half a dozen times, working out who would play and sing what. They didn't have a chance to work with the rest of the band, so they decided they would end the set playing it as a duet.

Between them, they were able to figure out what songs everyone knew, so they had some chance of sounding like a real band. Jimmy decided what song he wanted to open with and handed the set list to Buddy, who took it out to go over it with the rest of the band. Buddy seemed sure they would show up, so Jimmy stopped worrying about it.

Jimmy changed into his stage outfit, which differed little from what he had been wearing all day. A small closet in one corner of the room held all the costumes Jimmy had ever worn on stage, from the bell bottoms and floral print shirts to the platform shoes and tight pants he had worn a grand total of one time, in a disastrous 1976 attempt to play that funky music. He settled on a sleeveless black T-shirt with *The Black Velvets* emblazoned in silver across the front, and *The Loudest Bar Band in the World* across the back. He slipped on his favorite faded pair of Levi 501s, then pulled on his black motorcycle boots. *Ready to rock.*

Buddy opened the door. Jimmy peeked out at the crowd and felt his stomach clench. He was used to looking out at an empty dance floor. The club that he expected might hold a few hundred bodies was overrun with thousands of people, milling about, talking, ready for a show. Jimmy couldn't recognize a lot of the people, but some. There were Keith Moon and John Bonham in an animated discussion, mimicking drum licks. A few feet away, Karen Carpenter was laughing at something

Ricky Nelson had just said. Behind them, Jim Morrison, Bobby Darin and John Lennon were talking together, lost in their own conversation. Jimmy felt his knees weaken. He barely made it to the chair.

John Lennon. There’s a freakin' Beatle in the crowd, and I’m supposed to play? I saw Jimi Hendrix out there. He was the most creative guitarist I’ve ever seen. How can I play my little licks in front of him? I’m not even a shadow of their greatness.

He tried to calm his nerves with the same vocal warm-up routine he’d always done before a show. “Eeeeeeeh. Aaaaaaaaaaah. Eeeeeeeeh. Aaaaaaaaah. Rrrrrrrolling on the Rrrrrriver." He cracked his neck left, then right, put his hand on his diaphragm and sang, “I am Jimmy Velvet. Everyone else is playing for second best,” until he had pushed all the air out. He rolled his shoulders and decided he was as ready as he would ever be. Right then, Buddy stuck his head in the door, laughing bespectacled eyes alight with excitement.

“Are you ready, headliner? I think they’re gonna tear your new place down if we don’t go on pretty quick.”

Jimmy slipped the Stratocaster's strap around his shoulders. “I guess I’m as ready as I’m ever going to be.” *Actually, I think I might throw up. But best not to say it.*

“Hang on a second,” Buddy said. “I know you’re scared. I get that. But listen, you’re about to rock those people’s worlds. When we sing our song—our *new* song—man oh man,” Buddy whistled long and low, “look out. I’m not sure what’s going to happen, but I’ve got a feeling it’s going to be big.”

Jimmy laughed a little and said, “Buddy. You’re not helping me feel less nervous, you know. Let’s go do this thing.”

“Let’s rip ‘er up,” Buddy agreed, and they walked out of the dressing room to the backstage area. Dennis Wilson, Jon Averill, Roy Orbison, Janis Joplin, Sam Cooke, Elvis #17 and Uncle Bill were waiting for them. Dennis was spinning his drumsticks. Jon was nervously running his fingers over the strings of his bass, and Janis was whispering something funny in Roy’s ear.

"I'm going to let them know we're ready to go," Buddy said.

Jon said, "Dude, I thought you'd be younger by now. Are you staying old?"

Jimmy nodded and said, "Yeah, I feel great, but I've kind of gotten used to these wrinkles and gray hair. I think it makes me look kind of distinguished."

"It makes you look like my dad," Jon said, smiling. "Break a leg, Mr. Velvet."

Jimmy went to the young Elvis. "Hey, I'm glad you made it. Did you see the set list? There's a couple of them on there that I hoped you'd sing with me, especially *That's All Right.* I figure since you play the young Elvis, it should be right in your wheelhouse."

Dennis Wilson snickered a little bit and said "Shit, man…"

Jimmy looked from face to face. No one was making eye contact. *Everyone's in on a joke but me.* "What? What's going on?"

Everyone looked at #17, but no one said a word.

Elvis looked at the ground for a heartbeat, two, then looked up with that unmistakable Elvis grin. "Uh, yeah, about that. Ah'm not really Elvis 17. Ah'm Elvis Presley. It's a pleasure to meet you."

Jimmy felt a shiver run down his back. *Elvis Presley.* Then he thought back on the conversation he'd had with what he'd taken for just another Elvis impersonator. *Oh, shit.*

"Ah'm sorry, man," Elvis continued. "Ah know Ah shouldn't do that to people, but Ah just can't help it. If Ah tell people Ah'm Elvis, they get all freaked out and start stutterin' and stammerin', but if they think Ah'm just an impersonator, we can have a real conversation. Sometimes that big castle's more of a prison than a home. Anyway, Ah really am sorry."

Jimmy blew out a big breath. "No, don't worry about it, I just hope I didn't…"

"Oh," Elvis said, "You were worried that Ah might be upset because you said that mostly all Ah played for was blue-haired ladies? Nah, Ah don't even remember you sayin' that!" He winked at Jimmy and slapped him on the arm.

Now I get it. The Elvis magic. Incredible good looks, aw-shucks demeanor, and an endless supply of charisma. It charmed a world and changed the history of rock 'n roll.

"Well, as long as you don't even remember that…" Jimmy said, smiling. Dennis, Roy and Janis all laughed.

Buddy came back, flashed them a thumbs up, and the lights went down. Everyone made his or her way out onto the stage. Dennis clambered behind his drum kit, Jon plugged into his bass amp, and Jimmy and Buddy did the same with their Stratocasters. Elvis had his Ebony Gibson Dove acoustic with "Elvis Presley" in script on the neck strapped on and ready to go. Roy stood behind three microphone stands as part of the most ridiculously illustrious backup vocal group in rock 'n roll history: himself, Sam Cooke and Janis Joplin.

The crowd chatter quieted until the only sounds were clothes rustling and shoes scuffing against the dance floor. A single spotlight engaged with a *thunk*, pinning Jimmy to the center stage.

Tentatively, Jimmy stepped forward to the mic and said, "Hello, Rock 'n Roll Heaven, I'm Jimmy Velvet. Thank you for being here."

Applause rippled through the crowd. Bic lighters flicked on all through the house. Jimmy blew them out with the distorted, feedback-heavy intro of Norman Greenbaum's *Spirit in the Sky*. The noise doubled, then tripled. When it was time for the first verse, Buddy nodded to Jimmy, as if to say *It's your night. Take it.*

As soon as he started to sing, the oddness of the situation, who he was playing with, who he was playing for, melted away. He could have been back at *The Dew Drop Inn* in Pendleton, Oregon, or the *Astor Park* in Seattle, or any of a hundred places he had played in his career. Everything but the rhythm, the melody, the feeling of playing a great rock 'n roll riff faded out of existence. Buddy stepped to the center mic and sang the chorus with Jimmy and Roy while Sam and Janis provided the call-back vocals and hand claps. When Jimmy finally allowed himself to step out of his reverie for a glance at the crowd, he saw they were raising their hands, clapping along and stomping their feet.

Jimmy dropped to one knee and blasted the final power chord before segueing directly into *Radar Love.* Dennis Wilson laid down the snare drum beat and Jimmy stepped to the microphone and said, "Ladies and gentlemen, may I introduce to you Mr. Jon Averill on the bass." Jon took two steps forward and laid down the rock-solid bass line that propelled the song forward.

The crowd never sat or quieted down as the songs flowed one into another: *Helter Skelter, Knockin' on Heaven's Door, You Really Got Me* and *I Wanna Be Sedated.* Buddy handled the vocals on that last one. *Buddy Holly's hiccupy, staccato delivery on a Ramones song. Amazing.*

They did an early rockabilly set in which Buddy, Jimmy and Elvis all shared the microphone on *Good Rockin' Tonight, Rock Around with Ollie Vee* and *That's All Right, Mama.* Roy Orbison even stepped out of the background and sang *Ooby Dooby.*

I might look like an old man, but I sure don't feel like it. I feel like I could play forever.

At some point, members of the audience started jumping up onstage and jamming on songs. For a while, the set list went out the window. Otis Redding was first, joining Jimmy and the band on a blistering version of *Respect.* That opened the floodgates. Danny Rapp jumped up and reminded everyone that *Rock 'n Roll is Here to Stay.* For a while, John "Gonzo" Bonham took over the drum set for Dennis Wilson, who joined the back-row vocalists and chipped in harmonies. Freddie Mercury, looking young and strong, strutted across the stage and tore into *Good Golly Miss Molly.* Jackie Wilson, Johnny Burnette and Del Shannon followed.

Jimmy slowed things down for a few minutes and asked

Karen Carpenter to come up and sing *Goodbye to Love*, explaining that he'd always loved the guitar solo in the middle. Karen Carpenter, Dennis Wilson, Roy Orbison and Sam Cooke harmonizing while Jimmy and Buddy traded guitar licks was too good to have ever been heard on earth, but it was perfection in Rock 'n Roll Heaven.

Jimmy turned to his Uncle Bill, standing almost forgotten at the back of the stage, and motioned him to come forward.

"One of the best things about tonight is that I get to share it with family. This is my uncle, Bill Andrzejewski. I love him, because he's my uncle, of course, but he gave me the greatest gift anyone ever could have." Jimmy lifted his Strat over his head and saw that someone was handing him his Epiphone. He lifted it high up. The spotlight followed, playing reflections from the polished surface across the crowd. "He gave me my first guitar. He gave me music."

The crowd roared, then quieted as Jimmy slipped the guitar on and played the chords to *I'm so Lonesome I Could Cry.* No flash or showing off, Jimmy played the clip-clop chords the same way he had sitting with Bill on the bottom bunk in his bedroom on his tenth birthday.

He nodded to Bill, who stepped up and offered a very credible vocal, even though his voice was thick with emotion. The crowd was silent for the song, but erupted in applause as the final note faded. After that, Jimmy announced: "It's been such an honor to be here and play for you. We've got a couple more special things lined up to close things out tonight…"

Cries of "No, not yet!" and "More!" rang out through the crowd.

"... before we leave, I want to turn the microphone over to Mr. Sam Cooke, because *A Change is Gonna Come!"*

They didn't have a string section to handle the intro, so Sam stepped up and delivered it in pitch-perfect *a cappella*.

At the end of the first verse, Jimmy waved Roy Orbison and Elvis Presley to the front of the stage and they backed Sam's lead with three-part harmony. Much of the crowd joined in and sang the last chorus with them. Jimmy slung his guitar around behind him and performed like a conductor, leading everyone through the finish. As the final words echoed off the walls, there was a silent moment, then deafening cheers.

Jimmy switched back to his Strat, then gave a signal to Jon, who stepped forward and laid down the rolling groove that kicked off *Rock 'n Roll Boogaloo,* the closest thing to a hit single The Black Velvets ever had. With the bass line throbbing, Jimmy approached the mic and said, "I know you might have never heard this song, but Jon and I wrote it a long time ago. I hope you like it."

The crowd roared its approval, and by the time they sang the infectious, hook-filled chorus of "So won't you, won't you do, the rock 'n roll Boogaloo, with me," the crowd was singing along again. It might not have had the depth and meaning of *A Change is Gonna Come,* but sometimes rock 'n roll music is just about having a good time.

When Jimmy did his last windmill jam of the night on the final power chord, the crowd was so loud that Jimmy felt the floor shake. The rest of the band came to the front of the stage. Everyone put arms around each other and took a deep bow.

He looked up to see the whole crowd smiling, screaming and stomping their approval. Clear at the back of the crowd, where he would be hidden if he wasn't so tall, was Pertime.

He was smiling and clapping along.

Chapter Fourteen

The band ran offstage together, sweating, laughing and pounding each other on the back.

"What a show!" said Elvis.

"I don't know if I've ever heard a crowd so loud," Janis said at the same time. It was a little hard to hear what was being said, between everyone talking at once and the crowd stomping and chanting "Encore, encore, encore!"

Buddy peeked around the corner of the stage and said to Jimmy, "I think we better towel off and go back out there before they tear your brand new place down to the studs."

Jimmy nodded and threw Buddy a towel. They both grabbed their acoustics—Buddy's Gibson, Jimmy's Epiphone—and walked back on stage. When the spotlight flipped on to follow them, it was the one thing that could make the crowd even louder.

The stage had been cleared of everything except for two stools and two mic stands. Jimmy and Buddy sat down, adjusted the microphone heights, and strummed a couple of chords, which quieted the crowd. *Something's in the air. I know it. So do they.*

"Thank you," Jimmy said. "I played most of my life in dive bars and saw a lot of empty dance floors, so I can't tell you how much it means to me to have this chance to play for you tonight."

The crowd broke into loud applause again. A woman's voice yelled "We love you, Jimmy!"

Jimmy laughed and shook his head a little. "I love you too. All of you. Thank you for making me feel so welcome tonight. It's more than I ever expected." He paused for a moment, glancing at Buddy and gathering his thoughts. "There's been a lot that's surprised me recently. First, I was a little surprised to die…" A few chuckles and nods sprinkled through the crowd. "…and then I was surprised to open my eyes again." More nods.

"What surprised me the most, though, is that no one here has been able to make new music or create something new in any way. That feels so wrong to me."

Grumbles of agreement rose from every corner of the audience.

"I messed up so much in my life. I had a beautiful daughter. I barely ever saw her. The best woman I ever met loved me truly. I pushed her away. It's too late to change any of that, but it's not too late to do things right here. For me, that means using the gifts that God gave us. Part of that gift is creating something that's never been heard before. That's what Buddy and I have done tonight, and we want to share it with you now. It's called *Edge of Heaven.*

Jimmy nodded at Buddy, who played the lead guitar part they had created in the dressing room. Jimmy joined in on rhythm. The crowd hushed, turning their heads to absorb the sound, trying to see if they recognized it.

Jimmy leaned into the mic and sang, softly at first, then building:

Standing on a stage close to heaven
My heart on my sleeve
My guitar in my hand
Cheers ring so loud
From the colossal crowd

But when the curtain goes up
Will they hear what I play?
When the curtain goes up
Will I hear what I say?

Through this storm of emotion
All the thunder and lightning
Make those broken down bus rides
Through the long dark night seem
Like a time that has finally passed

At the chorus, Buddy began harmonizing with Jimmy:

Though many times I was wrong
Now it's all right, at last
I've struggled to the end of the fight
Always keeping my sight
Firmly fixed on the one true light

They sang the chorus twice, their voices rising in harmony each time they sang "one true light." The crowd was quiet except for a few whispered exchanges.

Jimmy sang the next verse alone:

Sometimes I stumbled from the path and went astray
Some of those choices I made
Well, they turned out the wrong way
And happiness just vanished like smoke
Leaving the pain of trying to fix
What I so easily broke
That happy union that brought life to a girl
I made a mess out of that
And now they're back in their world
A world without me
I came here with regrets
That there wasn't enough time

Tears streamed down Jimmy's face as he remembered that picture of Emily, floating in the water in front of his face. His voice broke as he and Buddy stopped playing. They reached out and put their hands on each other's shoulders. Buddy leaned over to Jimmy's mic, and together they sang the chorus one last time, *a cappella*:

Many times I was wrong
But now it's all right,
I've struggled to the end of the fight
Always keeping my sight
Firmly fixed on the one true light

Jimmy bowed his head, exhausted.

Jimmy's Real Rock 'n Roll was silent for a heartbeat, then erupted in a cheer so loud it woke people up in Poet Heaven, Novelist Heaven and even sparsely populated Political Heaven. It continued on and on, washing over Buddy and Jimmy, who sat motionless on the stools. Finally they stood, smiled a little wearily, and waved to the crowd.

Buddy took the microphone and said, "Thank you. It's a new day in Rock 'n Roll Heaven. The scales have fallen from my eyes, as the preacher man used to say back in Lubbock. I just met Jimmy today, but I owe him so much. It's a tradition here in Rock 'n Roll Heaven that every headliner does one song all alone, so for the last time this evening, I am proud to present the newest member of Rock 'n Roll Heaven, Jimmy 'Guitar' Velvet."

Buddy walked off to thunderous applause, leaving Jimmy alone. The lights were all darkened except for the pure white beam illuminating him on the stage. He hadn't planned what this song should be. *Okay, I know what it is, but this is the wrong guitar.* He turned to go off stage, but there stood the most famous stagehand of all time, Elvis Presley, holding his Stratocaster out to him with a smile and a wink. Jimmy nodded his thanks, handed off his Epiphone and strapped on his Strat. *Together again.*

He stepped back to the microphone and said, "I used to tell everybody I wanted to have this song played at my funeral. As I think you can all understand, that's pretty silly, since I won't be there to hear it. I'm gonna play it for you now."

He pulled a pick off the mic stand and plucked the guitar intro to *Simple Man* by Lynyrd Skynyrd. The song had always reverberated in his soul, and he sang it with no thought for his vocal cords, shredding at will. The audience swayed back and forth to the rhythm of the song.

Ronnie Van Zant, now at the front of the crowd, smiled and nodded his benediction.

The spotlight shone straight into Jimmy's eyes, clear to the back of his skull. He turned his head left, then right as he played, but no matter where he looked, the searing brightness of the light shone directly through him.

He went down on one knee to play the guitar solo he had played so often, but found that both his head and his hands were betraying him. His head was swirling like a bad acid trip. His hands became clumsy and refused to find the right chords. He tried to stand and realized that all the strength had drained from his legs.

He sat down, then laid down. Even flat on his back, with his eyes squeezed shut, the light was there.

He squinted his eyes open a slit and saw that Buddy, Elvis and Roy were surrounding him. He tried to speak, or think, but had nearly no control over his body. Over Buddy's shoulder, Pertime appeared, wearing his Sunday Best and a placid smile.

Buddy put his hand gently under Jimmy's head and said, "Don't fight it. It's okay. It's going to be fine." He stood up, grabbed the microphone and said, "They're taking Jimmy back. He's done so much for us, let's give him a Rock 'n Roll Heaven sendoff he'll never forget!" He kneeled next to Jimmy again. His eyes were kind as he said, "Jimmy, we can't stop this, but remember us. We'll be right here when you get back. We'll never forget what you've done for us."

Jimmy 'Guitar' Velvet closed his eyes.

He fell through utter darkness.

Chapter Fifteen

Jimmy opened his eyes.

Where is everybody? Buddy? Elvis?

He saw flashing blue and red lights and heard the rush of water. He smelled mud and wet grass.

"Jimmy? Jimmy! You're back! Man oh man, I thought we lost you. You had no pulse, we did CPR on you for what felt like hours."

Rollie.

"When you didn't make it up, I went back in after you. Goddamn, I've never been so scared in my life."

If that's Rollie, then I'm...

"Excuse me, I want to take his blood pressure before we move him to the hospital."

Jimmy tried to focus on the new voice, but the world wouldn't stop spinning. A blue uniform loomed over him and put a blood pressure cuff around his left arm, inflating it while listening to a stethoscope.

"You're very lucky, sir. If this man here," he said, nodding his head at Rollie, "hadn't dove back in after you, you'd have been a goner for sure."

The EMT's face came into focus. It was familiar.

"Pertime?" It was the first word Jimmy had managed to get out.

The EMT smiled and said, "Excuse me?"

"Pertime, is that you?"

"Per…tine? No sir, I'm Dave. Do you remember receiving a bump on the head in the crash? Did you lose consciousness before you swallowed the water?" He shone a small flashlight first in Jimmy's right eye, then his left. He looked at Rollie and said, "Classic concussion symptoms. We're going to want to check him further at the hospital." Turning back to Jimmy, he said, "We're going to get you on a gurney and get you to the hospital in Lewiston. We'll give you a complete exam there." He stood up.

Just before he walked away, Jimmy would have sworn that Dave the EMT winked at him.

Chapter Sixteen
(Two Years Later)

Jimmy stood backstage at The Seattle Center Arena and craned his neck a bit so he could see the crowd. The opening act was finished; the house lights were up. Rollie had the roadies getting the Velvets' gear set up. Everything was in place.

Before Jimmy had drowned and come back, he never could have imagined this scene, but now it played out as often as he wanted. He turned around and said, "Glad this is the last show for awhile. I'm ready to get back to home life."

"I can add those to the list of words I never thought I'd hear you say, along with, 'You were right and I was wrong,'" said Debbie.

"Will you play my favorite song first, Daddy?" Emily asked. "Mom says I can't stay for the whole show, but I really want to see you do it."

Jimmy stuck his tongue out slightly at Debbie, then scooped up Emily, who squealed "Dad! Put me down! I'm too big to be picked up."

"You'll never be too big for your dad to pick you up," Jimmy said.

He looked into Debbie's eyes and his heart beat a little faster, just like always. He'd spent two years trying to rebuild the bridges he had burned so carelessly a decade before. He was making progress, but none of it came easily.

"So," he said to Emily, "what is this favorite song you want me to do? *Itsy Bitsy Spider? Row, Row, Row Your Boat?*"

"Daaaad. I'm not a kid any more. You know what song I want to hear."

"Okay, okay. I usually save that for the encore, but I'll do our version of *Simple Man* for that instead. You are a lot more important than…" he looked out at the audience again and pretended to count, "…four or five thousand of my new best friends."

When he had woken up on the bank of the Lashton River, Jimmy knew he'd received two impossibly precious gifts: perspective and a second chance. He had sworn not to waste either one. After spending a night at St. Joe's hospital in Lewiston, he'd called a band meeting and shown everyone a song he had written the night before, called *Edge of Heaven.*

Rollie had given him his *something about this is bullshit* look, and had kept asking him where he'd gotten it. He had trouble believing that Jimmy had written anything that good. Jimmy tried to pretend he was hurt, but couldn't manage it. Rollie was right. It *was* better than anything else he'd ever written.

The songs hadn't stopped coming, though. While Rollie was out finding another old bus with the insurance money, Jimmy went on a writing jag and produced enough material to fill an album. They recorded a demo of *Edge of Heaven,* and before they knew what was happening, they'd maneuvered that demo into a recording contract.

Six months later, The Black Velvets' debut album, *Rock 'n Roll Heaven,* debuted on the Billboard charts and *Edge of Heaven* made the Top 40. Critical reaction was surprisingly warm for a guy who still liked to describe himself as a "never-was." No less than Rolling Stone hailed it as "A rock 'n roll renaissance, parlaying the classic licks of the fifties, sixties and seventies into something that feels both new and seminal simultaneously."

Jimmy had seen these twenty-year "overnight successes" happen to dozens of other bands, but had long since stopped dreaming it might happen to him. As sweet as that was, he never lost focus on what was most important.

Emily.

No matter how much pressure the record company put on

him, he limited his tour commitments. In a few more years, if Emily stayed on teenage schedule, she would become embarrassed to be seen with him. He must make time for her now, or lose that time for good.

And that will not happen.

He used his first royalty check from the sales of *Rock 'n Roll Heaven* to buy a modest three-bedroom house in a nice part of Pocatello, a five-minute drive from where Debbie and Emily lived.

"We're ready," Rollie said. "Let's rock 'n roll!" He turned and ran as fast as Rollie ever did, to hia position at the sound board. He trusted no one else to manipulate the knobs that made Jimmy sound like he was supposed to.

"This is the last show for a while," Jimmy said. "So how about if you guys ride back to Idaho with us tomorrow? We've got plenty of room on the new and improved Magic Bus."

"No groupies going back home with you?" Debbie asked.

Jimmy smiled, held up three fingers like a boy scout, and said, "I promise. I've got this cute little blonde 'Pocatello girl' I'm working on. I think I might be making progress with her."

"Do you?" Debbie said, sweetly. "I'm still not much of a 'party with the band' sort of girl."

Jimmy sighed, leaned down and hugged Emily, then kissed her cheek. "Don't watch too many Rugrats episodes tonight, we've got a long trip ahead of us tomorrow."

"Rugrats? That's a baby show. I like Ren and Stimpy now."

Jimmy wanted to ask "Ren and who?" but he didn't. Instead he said: "Just go to bed when mom tells you to, okay? I love you, Em-bug."

"I love you too, Daddy." Emily put her arms around his neck and hugged him hard.

The house lights dimmed and Jimmy walked onstage. An unseen announcer said, "Seattle, are you ready? Welcome back the great Pacific Northwest's own Jimmy 'Guitar' Velvet and The Black Velvets!"

The crowd stomped, whistled and screamed. Fans held Bic lighters aloft, flames wavering.

This is what I've always dreamed about.

He looked offstage. Debbie and Emily smiled and waved.

They are what I've always needed.

Jimmy stepped to the microphone at center stage and said, "Buddy, this one's for you," before playing the now-famous opening riff to *Edge of Heaven.*

Author’s Note

My author’s notes have traditionally been pretty brief. A quick perspective on where the story came from, what it means to me, and we’re done. This one might be a bit longer, so I appreciate that you didn’t click back to the home page on your Kindle or slam the book shut as soon as I wrapped up Jimmy Velvet’s story. It means a lot to me that you've read this story, and even more that you’re sticking around so we can talk a bit more.

One of the questions any author gets asked is, “Where did you get the idea for this story?” Often I can’t answer that, because I don’t know. With this one, I do. This story took shape in my brain in the spring of 1993. I had just quit a pretty good job and was staying home taking care of my two daughters Desi and Samy. (Daughter #3, Sabrina, wouldn’t put in an appearance for another year.) Money was a little tight, but I had just splurged on a hardback copy of Stephen King’s *Nightmares and Dreamscapes.* That fell under the category of a major purchase at the time, but a new book from SK was a cause for celebration in my life. I had started reading him when I found a copy of *Carrie* in high school and had never stopped. He was, and is, my favorite writer.

Nightmares and Dreamscapes wasn’t a novel, but a collection of short stories and novellas. I am a fan of shorter fiction. In my view, Mr. King is a master of the form. One of the stories was called *You Know They Got a Hell of a Band.* As a former disc jockey and life-long music geek, I immediately recognized that as a line from the song *Rock ‘n Roll Heaven,* originally performed by the band Climax, but made famous by the Righteous Brothers. As soon as I saw the title, I got a little frisson of anticipation.

My favorite writer and my favorite subject—rock ‘n roll—together at last. I envisioned what the story was going to be.

I shouldn't have been so surprised to discover that Mr. King had decided to write his own story, not the one that was in my head. It was good, but definitely not the story I had envisioned. For the first time in my life, I felt inspired to sit down at a keyboard and write. Within twenty-four hours, I had completed the very first version of my vision of that story, which I called *Rock 'n Roll Heaven.* It was a 10,000-word short story, and I thought it was pretty good. It had a lot of the same elements as the story you just read: Jimmy Velvet, Buddy Holly and Pertime (his name came to me in a dream that night) were all there. Jimmy arrived in Rock 'n Roll Heaven via a bus crash, just as he did here.

1993 was a very different time than 2014 in many ways, though, including the publishing industry. Twenty years ago, if you wrote a 10,000-word short story, you could submit it to the gatekeepers of the few places that accepted stories of that length, or you could stick it in a drawer and forget about it.

I split Option #2, sticking it in a drawer but failing to forget about Jimmy, Buddy, Pertime, and Rock 'n Roll Heaven. In the intervening years, I would let my mind wander there and think about what that world would be like. I admit I liked spending time there. It was often more pleasant than real life.

In 2012, I self-published a book called *Feels Like the First Time*. That book told the story of how I met and fell in love with the literal girl next door in Mossyrock, Washington back in the seventies. It was a sweet love story that seemed to resonate with a lot of people. I sold and gave away a lot of copies of that book; there are over 130,000 copies of that book on people's Kindles and iPads. I saw the chance to be what I had always wanted to be: a storyteller.

It wouldn't do to waste it.

First, I resurrected another short story I had drafted in 1993, *Lucky Man.* It was the story of a former big-man-on-campus and of revenge served very cold. I considered expanding it and making it a novella or a novel, but chose to keep the scale small as a short story.

I wrote *Both Sides Now*, the non-fiction sequel to my first book, which officially left my autobiographical non-fiction cupboard bare. It was time for a first full-length fiction book, and it could only be one story: *Rock 'n Roll Heaven.* That's why this story feels so special to me—I've lived with it for more than twenty years before finally committing it fully to the written word.

The writing process brought some challenges unique to this story, first of which was "avoid getting sued." That meant fastidiously avoiding quoting any of the lyrics of the great songs I wrote about in the book. It would have been much easier to include the lyrics, but I did my best to bring the music to life without them. For one scene, though, I needed lyrics to convey the message.

No problem. I'll just write the song myself. How hard can it be?

Regardless of what you might think of me as an author or novelist, I can assure you that I am neither a songwriter nor a poet. I tried; in fact, I tried very hard, but my lyrics were abysmal. I refused to ruin what I considered a pretty good story by polluting it with stupid song lyrics. My much-loved older sister and key inspiration, Terri, had given me some great advice before she passed away. A portion of that advice was this: *use the other guy's brain*.

I took that to heart and reached out to an old friend of mine, Steve Larson. My most dedicated readers (bless you) may recognize that name as one of the two main characters in *Second Chance Christmas* and *Second Chance Valentines.* That is not a coincidence. I named that character after my friend, as I am occasionally wont to do. I sent Steve my pathetic lyrics and what I was actually hoping to accomplish with them and asked if he could maybe…fix them?

Being the very good man he is, Steve did much better. He took the essence of what I wanted and wrote an entirely new song for me, which now shows up as *Edge of Heaven* in the pivotal scene near the end of the story. I owe Steve for a lot over the years, but my debt increased dramatically when he gave me the gift of using those lyrics. With any luck, one of these days Steve will put some music to the lyrics, and I will be able to share the entire song.

In addition to the lyrics of *Edge of Heaven,* Steve also helped me with a lot of the guitar knowledge that is on display in the book. My fellow writer David Scroggins also gave of his time and wisdom in sharing a lifetime's history and love for guitars. Without them, I'm sure I would have made a bigger fool of myself than I did when it came to rock's mightiest instrument. (Sit down, drummers and bass players.) Whatever errors remain are mine alone, I assure you.

One final issue was deciding which rock 'n roll legends to include in the book. It is a fairly short story, so there wasn't room for everyone. I had a core list I knew I wanted to include: Buddy Holly (I think of the story as being about him, more than anything) Elvis Presley, Jim Morrison and Janis Joplin. That left a long list of artists who deserved a slot, but there was only room for a few of them. That is why some of the greatest rockers of all time got short shrift: Jimi Hendrix, Keith Moon, John Lennon, John Bonham and many more. To simplify the process a little, I set the story in 1993, meaning that legends like Kurt Cobain, Jerry Garcia, Johnny Cash and any number of other icons were still playing on Earth at the time the story took place. If I left one of your favorites out, please feel free to do what I did when I read Stephen King's story – write the one that is in your head. There's always room for another great rock 'n roll story.

Music—especially the music of the '50s, '60s and '70s—has always been a driving force in my life. I hope that the love and admiration I feel for the musicians who created that music came through in this story.

For me, at least, authorship is a collaborative partnership. My publishing team consists of J.K. Kelley and Linda Boulanger.

J.K. has been with me since the very first book. I don't know what you as a reader think about what an editor does, but with J.K., I'll tell you this: take whatever that is, double it, then multiply it by about ten. That's the contribution he makes to all my stories, large and small. He is with me from first conception (he's already hearing about stories I hope to write in 2016) to the final comma I somehow manage to misplace. I call him *The Reader's Best Friend* because he makes everything I write a better experience for you.

Linda, of TreasureLine Books, is my cover and layout artist. She and I worked together to craft the eye-catching cover of Jimmy Velvet and the Golden Road for more than a year before we finally got the finished product you hold in your hands. In addition to the cover, she is the typesetter. She makes sure that the story looks like a book, not a jumble of misplaced lines and margins. She is an artist in all ways, and I can't imagine putting out a book without her.

Also invaluable and deserving of many thanks are my beta readers: Craig Worthington, Brad Raasch, Laura Heilman, Jeff Hunter, Karen Lichtenwalter, Heather Brush, Joni Furry and Cindy Rives. They generously gave their time to read this story in its roughest form and made a number of invaluable suggestions and contributions.

If you would like to join the ranks of my *Constant Readers,* you can sign up for my mailing list here: http://bit.ly/1cU1iS0. I only send you messages when I have a new book or story available and of course I would never sell your email address to anyone. If you sign up, you'll be among the first people in the world to know when I have a new story out and I'll even give you a discount for buying it early.

Thank you so much for being a reader. You bring the world I created to life.

Shawn Inmon
Enumclaw, Washington
March 2014

Bonus Section

Enjoy a short story
also written by Shawn Inmon

Nothing has ever gone wrong for Brett Mann - until tonight.

Lucky Man is the story of a Big Man on Campus returning to the site of his high school triumphs for his 25th Reunion. His life has been blessed with an elegant, beautiful wife, brilliant children, a career that is the envy of any man and more money than he can spend.

The real question is, did he really earn all that himself, or has he led a charmed life? Most importantly to him, is that charm about to become a curse?

Lucky Man

Often, over the years, in hallways and classrooms, Mirela would keep a surreptitious eye on him. No cheerleader she, the girl put off the risk of embarrassment and rejection until the clock of attraction came close to the stroke of midnight and she could wait no more. *Finally she resolved: it's the best weapon I've got. Now or never.*

Brett Mann emerged from Midland High School into the bright sunshine. Someone's car stereo was blasting Rick Astley's *Never Gonna Give You Up*, and he bobbed his head slightly to the beat of the song. Two more weeks, then graduation, and he could get the hell out of this little town God had dropped him in and start the life he knew was coming.

He'd broken up with his girlfriend Suzie the month before, considering her a potential anchor that might slow his escape from Midland's gravity pull. Lots of people talked about getting out of town when they graduated, but few got out and stayed gone. On reflection, he realized he might have dumped Suzie a little too early. He was, after all, a healthy, active 18-year-old boy. He had needs.

He was halfway up into the seat of his '81 Ford F150 when he heard a low feminine voice: "Hi, Brett."

He stepped down and turned around. The girl looked a little familiar, but he couldn't come up with her name. "Umm… hi?"

"I know we've never really talked before, but with Graduation coming up and all…"

Brett appraised her assets. Average height, average weight, not a bad body, but that nose, holy Jesus, what a beak. Still, it had been weeks. He could always just close his eyes. He gave her the same wolfish smile he had seen Tom Cruise flash in *Cocktail.*

"Anyway, I'm Mirela. We've had a ton of classes together. Freshman English, Literature of the Great Religions, Geometry, Calculus..."

"Yeah, sure, I remember you," he lied. "Right, Mirela. Great. So, you wanna go for a ride? I've got a few hours before I've got to be at work."

Mirela's face brightened in a smile that almost made her pretty. Almost. She climbed in the passenger side of the truck.

Brett pulled the F150 out of the school parking lot, throwing a little gravel. He drove them out of town—a short trip—and then circled around the familiar back roads. After a few minutes, he pulled down a side road and then turned onto yet another that wasn't much more than a trail. A couple hundred yards of pothole avoidance put them out of obvious public view.

He turned the engine off and turned to her, trying to look past her nose and just focus on what he wanted. He slid over against her. Her eyes went wide with fear, but she didn't move away. He put his arm around her shoulders and pulled her to him, kissing her hard. When he pulled his mouth away, she said "Oh, Brett. I've always hoped… I mean, I…"

He kissed her again, hard, mostly to shut her up. He reached down and unzipped her jeans, and again she didn't stop him. Before she knew what was really happening, Brett's jeans were around his knees. Losing your virginity in the front seat of an F150 is unlikely to ever be graceful or romantic, and it was no exception for Mirela. After just a few moments of increasingly frenzied thrusting, Brett groaned and slid off her.

Less than a minute later, his jeans were buttoned up and he had begun turning the truck around to heading back into town. He hadn't said a single word since she had gotten in his truck.

Back at the school, he pulled beside the lone car in the school parking lot, assuming that it was hers. He kept the truck in gear, eyes straight ahead.

"So, Brett," Mirela said, "are we going to see each other now? Are you going to call me?"

As if snapping out of a trance, he realized she was still sitting beside him.

"Oh, yeah. Of course I will. I'll call you soon."

"OK. Well, 'bye, then."

Mirela waited a second as if for a kiss, then realized it wasn't coming and climbed out of the truck. Before she could find her keys and unlock her car door, he was gone.

Brett saw Mirela in the halls several times over the next two weeks, trying to avoid eye contact. When she did manage to catch his eye, he acted as though he didn't recognize her. He graduated, left town, and got on with life, just as he'd planned.

There would be better women, with better noses.

Brett spied a parking spot right by the front door of the school, pulling his restored '55 Corvette into the space. The blacktop was in poorer repair than he remembered, probably due to frequent maintenance levy failures. He showed his teeth in the rear view mirror, checking for stray food, then tucked his Dior sunglasses under the visor. Leaving the top down on the 'Vette, he straightened his tie, ran a hand through his thick hair and looked at the small crowd gathered by the front door. He smiled inwardly at the sagging physiques and bald heads of his former classmates. Over the door was a handmade sign: "Welcome MHS Class of '88."

Brett made it safely past the group without having to do much more than nod to a couple of people. He pulled open the double doors that led into the lobby of the school. *Why the hell did I even bother to come to this thing? There's no one here I care about ever seeing again.*

If he been more honest with himself, Brett would have admitted that he looked forward to the ego strokes that would come from returning home as a conquering hero. Instead, he told himself he did it as a commitment to his old school.

He walked to a table that had several rows of name tags, found his, and tried to decide where he could attach it without damaging his grey Dolce & Gabbana suit. A middle-aged bottle blonde materialized beside him, vaguely familiar.

"Brett. Brett Mann! I was hoping you would show up!" Her enthusiasm and volume, once virtues in an 18-year-old head cheerleader, weren't wearing well a quarter century on. Now she used too much makeup, and too obviously was fighting a desperate rearguard salon action against grey. *One more person trying too hard to hold on to something long gone.*

Brett let his eye wander discreetly down to the nametag affixed to her matronly bosom.

"Hello, Mindy." Brett flashed his shark's smile. "It's nice to see you."

"OMG, Brett, you too."

What middle-aged person is so pathetic as to speak aloud

in text-speak? He wasn't sure what his kids had replaced 'OMG' with, but he knew that by the time a phrase reached his ears, it was already out of style with Gen Y.

"You've been the talk of the Reunion Committee every time we've met," she gushed. "You're our most famous alumni."

Brett dimmed the wattage of his smile modestly.

"Oh, I guess I got lucky here and there."

"Lucky?" An octave higher. Mindy's voice was probably the bane of all dogs' existence. "Don't be so modest! The youngest CEO in the history of Consolidated Financial, married a supermodel, then you wrote that book... that book... oh, damn. What's it called?"

"*I'm Brilliant, You're Not Bad Yourself,*" he said, a bit miffed. *But why should she remember? She's probably never read anything more sophisticated than* People.

"That's right!" she said, clapping her hands. She was even enthusiastic that Brett remembered the title of his own book. "And that was a Best Seller, wasn't it?"

"Thirty-two weeks on the *New York Times* Best Seller list," he agreed. "The sequel, *I'm Still Brilliant, How About You?* will be out soon." Hearing footsteps, Brett looked over Mindy's shoulder and saw three Mindyesque middle-aged women rushing toward him, squealing. He felt a chill run up his spine as though someone had run over his grave. Before the overstuffed, over-rouged, over-everything trio could rehash the gushfest, Brett took action. "Excuse me, Mindy, I've got a really important phone call I've got to take," he said, making a dash for the boys' bathroom just down the hall. He closed the door behind him with a whoosh and leaned against it, letting out a sigh of relief.

"Attack of the cheerleaders, huh?"

Brett had thought he was alone, but looked up to see a beefy, red-faced man smiling at him.

"Sorry, didn't mean to scare ya. I'm Bill. Bill Stinson," he said, extending a hand the size of a catcher's mitt. I didn't go to school here, I just married into it." He laughed at his wit.

"Pleased to meet you, Bill. I'm Brett Mann."

"Didn't mean to interrupt, Brett. I'll leave ya to it," the large man said, leaving the bathroom, still chuckling. This was going to be eternity in an afternoon.

Brett walked to the basin, turned the cold water on and splashed it on his face, glancing at his reflection in the same mirror he had used decades earlier. He waggled his eyebrows slightly at himself, satisfied, and tested the new cell phone app he had downloaded. It made his phone ring with a touch of the power button: the perfect social parachute for bailing out of banal conversations with forgettable ex-classmates.

He cracked the door open slightly, peeking out to make sure that Mindy's posse had found some other ball of yarn to play with. They had. Smoothing the wrinkles from his jacket front, he put his game face back on and stepped outside.

"Hello, Brett." A throaty contralto.

Jesus Christ, he thought. *Is everyone here a goddamned ninja?*

The woman who had spoken was standing slightly in the shadow of the lockers. All he could see was an enigmatic smile, but his first thought was that she was beautiful.

"Don't worry, I don't expect you to remember me," she said. "I'm Mirela Marko."

Brett felt his interest stirring. "Mirela Marko, Mirela Marko…" His memory lived down to her expectations. Who the hell was she? She moved out of the shadows. The beauty he had thought he had seen evaporated.

Fifty-foot pretty, five-foot ugly, he thought to himself. He reached in his pocket for his phone, ready to trigger the ring and escape.

She reached out and put a hand on his.

"Don't worry, I won't keep you long. You don't need to make a getaway."

Brett laughed hollowly, shaking his head as if that was the farthest thing from his mind.

"So, Brett, how's your life been?" She paused and smiled. When she smiled, she almost made it back to pretty. "Never mind, you don't need to answer, I already know. It's been great. Phenomenal. You have led a blessed life. In fact, that's exactly what you've done. I know, because that blessing came from me."

Nutjob alert, Brett thought.

"Uh, okay. Well, Mirela, it was really good to see you again…," Brett lied as he turned to leave, not bothering to fake his phone's ring. She put a firm hand on his shoulder, stopping him.

"You don't want to leave just yet, Brett. You need to hear what I have to say."

He narrowed his eyes and cocked his head at her, but stayed put.

"I know you don't remember me, and that's all right, because I remember you, and I've been waiting for this night for so long I can't believe it's finally here."

He took one small step away from her, but something kept him from going any farther.

"It's sad that you did so much to ruin my life, and you didn't even take notice of it, but by the end of tonight, all our scores will be settled." Her voice became eerily calm, rhythmic, confident, even enchanting. "Before the night is over, everything you hold dear will be gone. Your wife? Gone. Your beautiful twins? Gone. Your money, your career, your business? All gone. Even your precious face…" She trailed off, but the wistful smile on her face was downright creepy.

"You have no idea what you're talking about, and neither do I. I think you need therapy. You're right; I don't remember you. But if you ever threaten me, or my wife, or my children again, I will have you arrested." Even as he said it, it sounded hollow and lame.

"Oh, Brett, it's fine. You can go now," she said. "Go and lick the wounds you're about to get. But remember this: all the good things that have happened in your life were because I cursed you with perfect fortune. I wanted you to have known only goodness in your life. Now, when you need it, you have no ability to handle adversity."

"You're insane," he said, but a part of what she said rang true. He couldn't remember what it felt like to fail.

She smiled as if she could read his thoughts and they pleased her.

"I know you'll be wondering, so I want you to know right now that this isn't a negotiation. I'm not asking for anything from you, and I won't take anything from you. I do have one way out for you, but right now you think this is all bullshit, so I'll save that for later."

By the time she was about a dozen steps away, Brett had convinced himself that she was completely unhinged and belonged in a rubber room on medication. He massaged the back of his neck, shook his head, and blended in with a crowd of people moving toward the multipurpose room where dinner was to be served.

The room hadn't changed since he had eaten his last meal as a senior. Since some of his classmates probably worked in its kitchen by day, the food likely wouldn't have improved either. Row after row of folding tables with uncomfortable-looking benches filled the middle of the room. Framed pictures of every graduating class since the school had opened in 1952 lined the walls.

Brett walked along the tables until he saw his name on a place card. He slid gracefully into the bench seat, flashing his polymer smile at those nearby. The crazy woman grew less important and more pathetic with each minute. One last eye roll was all her memory deserved.

Someone was looking at him. "Oh, hello," he said with a trace of embarrassment.

"Hello… Brett," said a mousy brunette across from him, reading his name tag. *She doesn't recognize me? Wonder what cave she lives in.* "I'm Brenda."

"Very pleased to meet you," Brett said by rote. He was

already casting around the table looking for someone more interesting when the big fat guy from the men's room sat down next to Brenda. His eyes lit up when he recognized Brett.

"Hey, man, we've got to quit meeting like this, or our wives are gonna get suspicious." He laughed and made the sort of sound that gets a little less bearable every time you hear it.

Brett showed a tight smile, but couldn't even work up a pity chuckle.

"Honey," Bill said, "this is the guy I told you was hiding from the cheerleaders in the boy's john."

Brenda looked appraisingly at Brett and then away, disinterested. His lips tightened a bit more. He wasn't accustomed to being ignored by anyone, let alone a plain-Jane housewife in a flower print K-Mart dress.

When she looked back at him, she said softly, "While you're here, do you know where your beautiful wife is? I do. I know she's home, getting serviced by your personal trainer. In your own bed. Unlike you, she's enjoying herself."

Face flushed, Brett lost some of his cool. "What the hell is wrong with everyone here tonight? My wife couldn't be here because she's at a children's charity event!"

Both Brenda and Bill stared back without expression. Bill raised his eyebrows and shrugged in the 'you know how women are' universal male body language.

"I don't expect you to believe me," Brenda said. "Why don't you give her a call? See what she's up to?"

"Why don't you… Oh, forget it! Is everyone at this reunion crazy? I don't need to call my wife. She would never cheat on me." Brett stood up too fast, banging his knee on the table's underside. Fighting down the pain, he refused to limp as he walked away. The nearest exit, if he remembered correctly, was a set of side doors leading to blessed fresh air.

As the doors began to swing closed, he fished out his phone and dialed Monique. With the charity auction in full swing, his wife might not hear the ring, but even her voicemail greeting would be a reassurance.

While the phone rang and rang, images began surfacing from his subconscious mind, almost as if timed for just this moment. He thought about working out at the gym with Monique and Ted, his personal trainer. Ted was a triathlete in his mid-twenties, in better shape than Brett would ever be again. He also remembered the way Ted worked with Monique, spotting her as she lifted, changing the settings on the equipment, paying attention to her.

When her voicemail finally answered, it provided Brett no comfort at all. He spoke after the tone: "Monique, it's me. I'm having a crazy night, and I need to talk to you. Call me as soon as you get this."

He punched "End." On a whim, he dialed his home number.

After three rings, he heard the phone pick up. After several seconds of silence he heard a masculine voice answer "Hello?"

"This is Brett Mann. Who is this?"

Brett heard sounds like a hand trying to muffle the transmitter. He strained to hear, distantly: "Shit. It's your husband! I'm an idiot, I thought it was *my* phone…" It clicked dead.

He hit "Redial" and listened as the phone rang and rang, then eventually heard his own voice say "This is the home of the Mann family…" He hung up and called back, getting exactly the same response. He leaned against the cool brick of the building, trying to gather his thoughts and emotions.

"Screw it," he said, taking a deep breath.

The phone in his pocket vibrated. Now he would get some answers. A glance at the caller ID, though, told him that it was the office. Odd. "Brett Mann," he snapped.

"Hello, Brett, sorry to bother you. This is Rita." Her voice was worried and faded out at intervals.

Rita was Brett's executive secretary of fifteen years. She was in her mid-sixties, built like a piece of granite and just as dependable.

"Sorry, I'm having an unbelievably bad night. What's up?"

"I hate to make your night worse, but we've got serious trouble here at the office. I mean trouble like I've never seen before.

"Okay. Okay, hold on. What's going on?" Brett glanced at his watch. 7:15 on a Friday night. She often worked late, but this was an unlikely hour for any sort of crisis.

"I had just run the last of the quarterly reports and I was scanning them to your email and getting ready to lock up when two men came in. They asked for you, and when I told them you weren't here, they showed me a badge and a warrant and said they had a team on the way to search the office, including all records and computers."

"What?" Brett's baritone voice went falsetto. "What the hell? Who are they?"

"The badge said FBI, but they said they also had people from the IRS coming with them to conduct a forensic audit. They said they were setting up a base of operations and would be here for the duration. I don't know what to do; they aren't letting me near any of the computers. Can you get down here?"

"I can, but it's going to take me a few hours. I'm not in the city; I'm at my damned 25th high school reunion. I knew I shouldn't have come to this thing. Goddamn it, why did this have to happen tonight, when I'm a hundred miles from the city?"

In the back of his mind, he heard the contralto again. *Your money, your career, your business? Gone.*

He ran his hand through his hair and said, "Listen. I'm leaving here now. I'll be there in two hours. Keep them away from my office and especially my computer."

"I'll do my best, but these guys look serious and have Federal warrants. I'm afraid they'll throw me in jail. I love my job, but I can't do that, Brett…"

"Just… just… do what you can. I'll call the lawyers and get them down there as fast as possible to stop this bullshit. In the meantime, lock my office and tell them you don't have a key. I'm on my way." Brett ended the call and slipped his phone back into his pocket. He ducked back into the multipurpose room and saw that someone he didn't recognize was making a speech at the front of the room. He slipped along the back wall, trying not to be too obvious. He hit the double doors to the hallway with enough speed to make a satisfying thud.

The doors flew halfway open, then stopped with a thud of steel on flesh and bone. A feminine voice squealed in shock and pain. Brett drew up short by reflex and saw that he, the doors and Brenda Stinson had all tried to occupy the same space at the same time. She had a red mark on her forehead where the door had bonked her. The splash of two plastic cupfuls of Merlot all down the front of her dress made a rather larger red mark.

She looked down, saw the stain and started to cry. "I never get a new dress, and now when I do…" Only then did she look up to see who was responsible. "You!"

Brett didn't care how often Brenda was permitted to splurge at Wal-Mart, K-Mart or whatever mart she considered her couturier. He pushed past her just as Bill turned the corner and surveyed the scene. Now Bill's ruddy face flushed the kind of scarlet usually associated with rosacea attacks, and his formerly jovial expression was twisted in a sour knot.

"Sorry," Brett said casually to Bill. "We had a bit of a collision."

As a boxer, Bill's form left a lot to be desired. The swing started at his knees. With any warning at all, Brett could have easily backed away from it, but no one had ever before swung a fist at him in anger. First came a muffled, thudding crack as Bill's workingman fist broke the cartilage in Brett's nose, then a clang as Brett's head left a massive dent in locker #101.

As Brett began to black out, he heard Bill saying, "No, you stupid son of a bitch. *That* was a bit of a collision."

When Brett opened his eyes, he expected to see paramedics, or at least a crowd of concerned onlookers. Instead, he was alone where he had fallen. He started to get up, then felt enormously queasy and decided to roll over and vomit instead. He threw up everything but his toenails and still didn't feel any better. Too dizzy to stand, he laid back down. In the process, he managed to drag the right arm of his suit through his vomit. He remembered a feeling like this from long ago: waking up the morning after he'd pledged Betas during his freshman year. An isolated memory: a Tri-Delt from the night before, too drunk to consent or decline. Cheap beer in industrial quantities.

When he felt a bit of clarity start to return, he stood up, leaning heavily against the dented locker. The glow of a cigarette indicated that he wasn't alone after all. Mirela stepped out of the shadows wearing her tiny, mocking smile.

He reached deep inside for whatever reserves of strength he had left.

"There's no smoking on school grounds, you little mental case."

"Strange," answered Mirela. "I guessed you'd have come up with 'witch' or 'bitch.' You'd have been closer to the truth with either one."

"More likely both," he snarled. Her smile widened, but grew even colder.

"I think you're more open to listening to me now, aren't you, Brett?" She moved closer and reached a hand out, as if to gently probe his broken nose. He pulled his head away angrily, which sent another wrack of nausea through him.

With his eyes pressed nearly shut, he hissed, "What do you want from me?"

"For a big shot executive, you have a lousy memory. I told you before: I'm getting exactly what I want from you. There's nothing else you can give me. I don't need your money, and if I'd wanted to live the life you're living, I could have had that any time. Instead, I gave it to you. Now, I have one more gift for you."

She reached into her purse and pulled out a small pistol. Gripping it by the barrel, she offered it to Brett.

He glared at her suspiciously.

"It's all right. Take it. It's loaded with one bullet, but you can't hurt me with it anyway."

He reached out his shaking, bloody hand and snatched the gun away, immediately pointing it at her.

Mirela sighed. "Brett, Brett, Brett. Do you really think I would work this hard to ruin your life and then hand you a gun that you could use against me? Use your head. It is loaded, but it's as enchanted as your life has been until tonight. The only thing that bullet can do is put an end to your suffering."

His gun hand wavered, then sank toward the floor. "If you're saying I should use it to kill myself, you can go fuck yourself." Even to his own ears, he sounded like a petulant child.

"Very eloquent, Mr. Bestselling Author. But you're probably right, because I don't think you've got the guts to do it either. Especially since you seem to have left most of those on the floor," she added, taking a fastidious half-step back from the puddle.

"I really hope you don't kill yourself, and here's why. As bad as today has been for you–getting your nose smashed into a pulp, finding out your wife's having an affair, finding out you're being investigated for criminal fraud by the FBI and the IRS--"

"How...?" He caught himself. *I will not give her the satisfaction. I don't ever want to see that smug, creepy smile again, and I'm not going to play into her little game.*

"—but as bad as this day has been, this will be the best day of the rest of your miserable life. And here's the fun part! If you don't do yourself in by midnight tonight, I'm going to make it so that you can't escape by dying. In fact, if you survive the night, I can guarantee you that you will die a very old, lonely, miserable man."

She turned and walked a few steps down the hall before she turned and said "But be careful, Brett. There's only one bullet. Don't miss. You don't want to end up as a vegetable on top of everything else."

Brett suddenly sneezed toward the lockers, hosing a crimson spray onto #101 and #103. The explosion of pain made him weak in the knees. For a moment he felt like vomiting again, but fought it down as he put a hand on the locker to steady himself.

When his eyes focused again, she was gone. He weaved down the hall in the same direction she'd gone, which led to the parking lot. He tried desperately to conjure up a happy image of his own bed, softly lit by the glow of his bedside reading lamp. Instead, his mind's eye could only see an image of Monique riding Ted like it was the last race of the day at Churchill Downs.

He pushed that thought from his mind and remembered the conversation with Rita. He dialed her cell phone to see if the FBI and IRS had come back yet, and if they had gotten their hands on his personal computer. If they had, his next phone call might be to his lawyer from a holding cell, because there was enough on that hard drive to put him away for twenty years. The number rang and rang and eventually went into her voicemail.

"Goddamn it! Can't one goddamn thing go right for me tonight?" He bit his lip, realizing he was doing exactly what the little wacko had wanted him to do. He walked slowly outside and saw his car sitting right in front of the school, moonlight reflecting softly off its perfect body. The sight gave him strength and hope. That 'Vette would be the envy of any man. For a moment, he remembered who he was.

"I am Brett Fucking Mann. What the hell is wrong with me? I can figure all this out! Jesus Christ, I almost let that dumb bitch take over my mind. I can fix this. I can fix anything. I don't care what kind of a goddamned witch she is."

His phone vibrated and he looked at the screen, expecting to see that it was Rita or Monique calling him back. Instead, the caller ID showed an unavailable number. He took a deep breath, steeling himself for more bad news.

"Hello?"

Static distorted the female voice on the other end of the line. "…ello? Hello? This is… bercrombie. I'm trying to reach Brett Mann."

"This is him."

"Hello? This is the... I have... for Br... Mann. Is this...?"

"Jesus H. Christ," Brett said, raising his voice several notches, even though it cost him a blast of pain from his ruined nose. "This is Brett Mann!" he all but shouted.

"Oh. Mr. Mann, this is Officer Abercrombie with the State Patrol." The patrolwoman's voice conveyed somber sympathy even through the static and noise. "Can I ask where you are? I'd prefer to speak with you in person. I've been trying to reach your wife at home and on her cell phone as well, but she's not answering."

Brett stumbled forward, light-headed, feeling like he was about to pass out. Steadying himself with a large handprint on the Corvette's front bumper, he sat down on the curb.

"Please. I'm not in town right now. Please just tell me what's happened."

The silence stretched out for several seconds as Brett waited to see if he still had a life or not. For the first time in his adult life, he began to pray.

Just don't let it be Cheyenne and Avery. Not them. Please God, anything but my children.

"Mr. Mann... I would really prefer to talk to you in person. There... there's been an accident and I wish I could speak to you face to face. What I have to tell you is very difficult."

"Oh... no. No." His voice was a pleading whisper. Tears spilled down his face, mixing with the drying blood.

"Mr. Mann? There's been an accident, and I'm deeply sorry to inform you that both your children were seriously injured. There was very severe trauma. Neither survived..."

Officer Abercrombie kept talking, but Brett didn't hear her. His phone slipped from his grasp and clattered against the pavement. He blinked, trying to focus.

Memories swirled through his mind. Cheyenne at age two, jumping up and down on him, screaming "Body slam, Daddy, body slam!" Avery, chubby arms and legs pumping, running down the driveway and jumping into his arms.

Anything else, he could have survived. Maybe he was getting what he deserved with Monique cheating. Things had been distant between them for a long time, but he'd always thought there was time to fix things. *Your wife, gone.* And the truth was, he probably deserved whatever he got from the government. He had knowingly cut corners and done illegal things to get ahead. It had never bothered him, because it had never seemed like he was hurting anyone at the time, and he figured everyone was doing it. Most successful people probably did much worse. *Your money, your career, your business, gone.*

But this. There was nothing left after losing Cheyenne and Avery. He had always taken pride in being a good father. He had cared more for them than for houses, cars, boats, vacations, artwork, jewelry, or any of his other abundant possessions. Again he heard the witch's voice in his mind: *your beautiful twins, gone.*

The silver pistol weighed heavily in his pocket. He took it out and turned it over in his hand. It looked like the only cure for the overwhelming pain he was feeling.

He pulled the hammer back and placed the barrel under his chin.

He heard the witch's voice, chanting approvingly in his head, egging him on.

Don't miss, Brett. Don't miss...

In an exclusive neighborhood of Madison Park, just above Lake Washington, the Mann residence stood out in a neighborhood made up exclusively of properties designed to stand out. The yard lights out front glowed softly, casting pretty shadows against the rockwork. The frogs and crickets created a background serenade. All was quiet inside. Mrs. Mann had yet to return from her Children's Hospital charity dinner. The two 17-year-old Mann twins, Cheyenne and Avery, were already asleep in their rooms. They had to get up early for a backpacking trip the next morning.

Ninety miles south of Seattle, outside the multipurpose room of Midland High School, the night air was full of blasts of police chatter and blue and white lights. Midland High's Most Famous Graduate's body had long since been taken away in an ambulance. None of the Midland Police wanted to relinquish the biggest 'crime' scene in the town's history. They had heard that one or two of the Seattle stations were sending a reporter and camera crew, which hadn't happened since Mt. St. Helens had blown thirty-some years before.

Ten blocks away at the Stinson residence, Mirela Marko, Bill and Brenda Stinson and Mindy Parker sat around a table drinking coffee. Mirela wore a satisfied smile. "I know we rehearsed this dozens of times, but when the moment actually came, all I could think was 'He'll never buy this. He'll never actually believe I'm some sort of gypsy witch.' But then… he did. Unbelievable."

"You were perfect, Mirela," Brenda said. "Shit, I almost believed it myself toward the end."

"I couldn't believe it when you handed him the gun," Mindy said. "That was gutsy. He was so pissed by then that I was sure he was going to use it on you."

"By then," Mirela said, "I was so into the whole thing that I was just going for it. Hey, have any of you guys talked to Susan, Wayne, Jim or Alan? They were unbelievable. We never could have made this happen without them. I was listening to the asshole's end of the conversation when he was talking to his secretary and I could tell she believed they were the real deal. When he called his house and Alan answered the phone, I thought he was going to die. Which, I guess…" she said, letting the rest of the obvious thought trail away. "Hey, how did Alan manage to answer that call anyway? Did he break into the house?"

"No," Mindy said. "Remember, he works for Ma Bell. He directed all the calls to his own phone. Then, when he was done, he put it all back the way it was. They'll never be able to trace it."

"You know," Bill finally spoke, "I don't know what this guy did, but whatever it was, he pissed of the wrong bunch of girls."

"Much worse. He pissed off the wrong bunch of women," Mirela corrected, fixing him with a meaningful glare.

"Yes, he did," Bill agreed, quickly.

After a bit more small talk and speculation, Mirela and Mindy stood up. Both reached for jackets and purses. "I think it would be better if we all laid low for a while… didn't see or talk to each other," suggested Mindy. The Stinsons and Mirela nodded.

"Of course…" Mirela said, "there's always Jed Stevens. He was an asshole too." After a long moment's consideration, she said, "Oh well, I guess there's no hurry. We've got another reunion in five years."

Other Books and Stories by Shawn Inmon

Feels Like the First Time A heartfelt memoir of love found, lost and found again in small-town American in the 1970s. http://amzn.to/18Yj07m

Both Sides Now Every good love story deserves to be told from both sides. *Both Sides Now* is a companion book to the bestselling *Feels Like the First Time,* telling the story from Dawn's perspective. http://amzn.to/1bpmccM

Second Chance Christmas A second chance love story, combined with a Christmas miracle. http://amzn.to/1bjJGiV

Second Chance Valentines After reconnecting, Steve and Elizabeth face difficult questions about how to build from their new beginning. http://amzn.to/1dPdG49

Christmas Town A Christmas parable about the choices we make and what is truly important. http://amzn.to/1bYz7yE

Made in the USA
Columbia, SC
19 July 2022